Also by Natasha D. Frazier

Devotionals

I0586670

The Life Your Spirit Craves

Not Without You

The Life Your Spirit Craves for Mommies

Fiction

Love, Lies & Consequences

Through Thick & Thin: Love, Lies & Consequences Book 2

Shattered Vows: Love, Lies & Consequences Book 3

Non-fiction

How Long Are You Going to Wait?

Edited by: Cheryl Molin

Cover design by BJ Benjamin O'Neal (I Imagine Beyond)

For autographed copies, please visit:
www.natashafrazier.com

Note from the Author

I am thankful to my Heavenly Father, who has allowed me the opportunity to do the thing that brings me joy and peace and gives Him glory. This is book number 8! And we know that the number 8 represents new beginnings! I am so excited about this book because it is a little different than what I've written in the past. This is a heart warmer that will have you smiling and rooting for Kensi to find what she's looking for up until the very end.

God has given me a wonderful family who supports my writing career. Eddie, my awesome husband, I love you and appreciate you for all that you do. Thank you for your unwavering support. My babies: Eden, Ethan & Emilyn, mommy loves each of you dearly. To my mom, dad, stepdad and sisters, I thank you for your love and support. For my sister Courtney who doesn't want to be lumped in with everyone else, I love you and thank you for your support.

To my special set of girlfriends who push me to go further and have encouraged me from the very start: Tiera, Toccara & Shenitra - I love you ladies and appreciate your friendship. I consider myself blessed to be surrounded by such an awesome group of women.

Readers - Thank you for continuing on this literary journey with me. You each hold a special place in my heart, so please know that with every stroke of the keyboard, I am thinking of you. I hope this book makes you love a little harder and enjoy every moment of your life. The 5aithful 5abulous 5ive bookclub, BRAB, and others who have shown tremendous support, my heart swells with gratitude. Thank you!

Much love & many blessings,

Natasha

Kairos

The Perfect Time for Love

NATASHA D. FRAZIER

CHAPTER 1

Delight thyself also in the Lord: and he shall give thee the desires of thine heart. Commit thy way unto the Lord; trust also in him; and he shall bring it to pass. Those were the Scriptures that Kensi had chosen to live by, and her desires were simple: career progression and family. Today she was trusting God to bring one of those to pass. She could feel it in her bones; besides, she'd been positioning herself for this promotion since she was hired eight years ago.

Today was the day she'd dreamt about for the past few years—Kensi was certain of that fact as she strode into the editor-in-chief's office, dressed in her favorite burgundy colored suit with matching pumps, pearls around her neck and hair straightened down her back. She was dressed for the occasion. When she entered Mrs. Samantha Elkins' office, she accepted the bottled water offered to her, sat at the edge of her seat and crossed her legs at the ankles, excitement bottled up within her. She was ready. She smiled and nodded anxiously as her boss gave her accolades over her past assignments, one of which was the high-profile story of Joshua Archer's retirement from the NBA. Samantha Elkins' praise was nice, but Kensi's nods were intended to move her on to the good part—the part where they discussed her promotion.

"I'm impressed, Ms. Jacobson. You've outdone yourself this time and your efforts have not gone unnoticed." Samantha tapped the most recent issue of *The Big Apple Arts Chronicle* as she spoke.

"Thank you, ma'am." Kensi's response was rushed. She'd been rehearsing this scene in her mind all morning and it was moving much slower than she'd anticipated.

"And you know what this means, right?" Samantha smiled, waiting on Kensi's nod of confirmation. "I have an even more perfect assignment for you. You're so talented, Kensi, and the world of journalism could use more journalists with your skills, so you'll be working in Pepperton, Texas, training a few newly hired journalists for the *Pepperton Quad.* You'll also be covering Pepperton's Christmas celebration festivities, which I believe will be the perfect piece for our Christmas issue. Something new and refreshing," Samantha dramatized with her hands. "It's a lengthy assignment, but I know it's nothing that you can't handle," Samantha finished and handed the file to Kensi. With electronic media being a preferred method of communication for most, Samantha still preferred paper, as evidenced by the paper file she handed to Kensi; she needed something that she could *feel between her fingers,* she'd always said.

Kensi slowly reached for the file, waiting for the rest of the news. However, Samantha's attention had turned to her computer and it seemed that Kensi had been dismissed. Kensi stood to leave when Adam walked into Samantha's office, uninvited.

"What a great opportunity! Kensi, since you're leaving, I'd like to inform you that Adam is going to be our new assistant editor-in-chief!"

Kensi glanced from Adam to Samantha, attempting to mask the scowl, confusion, and disappointment that crept across her features. Was she supposed to offer congratulatory remarks?

"Give us a minute, will you, Adam?"

"Yes ma'am." Adam gave Kensi a pitiful look before turning to leave. He wanted to be the one to tell her about the promotion. He hated that she had to find out this way, especially since they were *more* than just coworkers.

"Sit down." Samantha gestured toward the seat that Kensi sat in just moments before.

Samantha rested her chin on her linked fingers. "Kensi, I know you've been working hard for the promotion, but you're so good in the field, and you have so much to offer and teach journalists who are just starting out. I know you may not see it just now, but this is going to be good for your career. Besides, I can't lose you in the field just yet—no one is as brilliant and resourceful as you!" Samantha worked to help Kensi see the best in the situation, but Kensi was not soothed by Samantha's compliments. She sat perched on the edge of her chair with stone-like features, clenching her teeth, to keep from bawling.

"You're disappointed, I know. But you're so great at what you do and you know I must groom Adam to take over the newspaper when I retire. He's my grandson and I must look after him and our family first. You do understand that, right?"

"No, no, I understand," Kensi stammered, attempting to keep her emotions and tears in check. But, she didn't understand. She'd worked far too hard for the position for it to be given to someone else just because he was a relative. And what made it worse is that she'd been dating Adam and he knew how much she wanted the position. He could have told her about it before now— but that was a situation she could fix.

"Who sends an employee on an extended assignment during the holiday season anyway?" Kensi fussed, though it was not unusual for her to travel during the holiday season because she had done so in the past. Yes, she was having a conversation with herself outside in the open, and she couldn't care less if someone saw her and thought she was losing her mind. Although it was about fifteen degrees and she was bundled up in her wool coat, scarf and gloves, she could still feel the heat rising on the back of her neck as she made the walk from the train station to her apartment.

Unlike the week-long work trips she was used to taking, this project was set to last at least a couple of months. When she arrived inside of her Manhattan studio apartment, she shrugged out of her coat and winter accessories and tossed them on the sofa. She headed straight for the closet and threw just about every piece of clothing she owned onto her bed. Wire hangers dangled in the closet. Pumps and the only pair of sneakers she owned were strewn across the floor.

This was not her idea of a promotion. She was so certain that she'd be up for the assistant chief editor position after breaking Joshua's NBA retirement story. Hands down, he was the best player in the league. Her story was perfect and included direct quotes from him that no other journalist had access to. And her reward was being shipped to some small town in Texas to train newly hired journalists and cover some small-town coach and his annual holiday event. Kensi and Samantha's ideas of career growth were on opposite ends of the spectrum.

Kensi had never even heard of Pepperton, Texas. In her mounting frustration, she hadn't taken the time to see how close Pepperton was to Houston. Maybe she'd be close enough to her best friend, Raegan, and that would make the situation a little more bearable.

If she had good sense, she would just quit and find a position at a newspaper or magazine that would value her resourcefulness, dedication and innate abilities.

The light but persistent tapping on her front door brought her inward battle to a halt. She had yanked the last few blouses off the hangers in frustration and now she tossed them onto the heap that lay on her bed. She took a couple of deep breaths and went to answer the door. Not giving much thought to the way she looked, hair disheveled, wrinkled pink T-shirt and a pair of yoga pants, she tiptoed to glance through the peephole at her uninvited guest. She quickly unlocked the deadbolt to allow her friend and coworker Adam access to her studio apartment.

"Ken-Ken, looks like you're almost ready to go?" Adam chuckled nervously as his eyes traveled to the pile of clothes on her bed. He stood with his hands planted in his pockets after giving her a tight squeeze, one that she didn't return.

"Something like that. You come by to say good riddance?" Kensi tossed over her shoulder, taking a few steps from the door to the refrigerator to grab a bottle of water. She offered one to Adam but he declined. He took a seat on the sofa and motioned for her to join him.

"I'm sorry. I know how much that promotion meant to you."

"Well, why didn't you turn it down when they gave it to you? That, my friend, would be showing me that you're sorry." She tilted the bottle in his direction before taking another sip.

"Would you have turned it down?"

"Heck no! But I wouldn't have showed up to your apartment apologizing either." Kensi eyed him carefully. "So, are you here to see if I've got beef with you?"

"I just want to make sure we're good, you know? I don't want this getting in between us." He smiled and tried to lean in for a kiss but Kensi leaned back and turned her head.

"Nah, we're good, but maybe we should cool it. I'm going away for a couple of months and there's no telling where I'll be going after that. I can't be certain of anything anymore." She may have been a little over dramatic, but she was confused; she thought the promotion was part of her path and now she didn't know what her next steps were going to be. She didn't have a plan B.

Adam didn't buy it. He leaned back and allowed his head to rest over the edge of the couch. He had seen this coming. Not because she was leaving, but because he had been given the promotion over her. This somehow validated Kensi's thoughts that no matter how hard she worked, they wouldn't see her as equal to any of the male journalists who worked alongside her. He cared for her, but his career was more important, so he acquiesced. Besides, how could he say no to "his Gigi"?

"Okay, well, I guess I'll see you around. Hug?"

This time Kensi leaned in for a hug. She did have feelings for him, and it seemed that their relationship was blossoming into something. But there was no way she could be with anyone who took her job, and no matter the circumstances surrounding Samantha choosing Adam over her, Kensi would only see it as Adam stealing her promotion and no room to trust him again. He was good, but he didn't deserve that promotion as much as she did, and Samantha knew that. This had more to do with keeping the company within her family, but Kensi didn't feel the need to spend energy trying to figure it out now.

She would make sure that she got her own promotion after this, even if it meant she had to go somewhere else.

CHAPTER 2

Where in the heck are they sending me? Kensi thought as she changed planes in Houston. She should have known something was up when she was directed to go to what seemed like the basement area of the airport. The crowd thinned the closer she walked toward that area. No more shops and only one terminal. It looked pitiful. When she neared the area, her eyes locked on a crop duster. *This has to be a joke,* she mused.

"Ma'am, am I in the right area?" she asked the airline representative, handing over her ticket.

"You sure are. Have a seat in the waiting area; we'll be boarding in just a moment."

That excuse for a plane told her all she needed to know about Pepperton. No one was there. Both Thanksgiving and Christmas were sure to turn out to be lonely. She'd give anything to be going home to her family instead of working this assignment, even though she hadn't been there in about two years and she'd have to deal with the questions regarding when she'd get married and have children. Even that had to be better than this situation.

After boarding, she had a flight of a little more than an hour to Pepperton. She pulled out the file her boss had given her and read it over, something she hadn't bothered to do before; she was too upset over not getting the promotion.

"This is nice, but I don't understand why it needs to be in a paper distributed in New York," she grumbled as she flipped through the pages. It was all about a small-town coach who dedicated time during the holiday season to bring the community together by hosting the town's Christmas extravaganza. She was about to close the file when a picture of the coach tumbled out of it and onto her lap. Dark eyes, flawless skin and perfect teeth. She even found the bald head and mole next to his right eye becoming. He was handsome. His smile was captivating.

She didn't realize that she was returning a smile to the image on the paper until the flight attendant interrupted her, asking if she wanted more peanuts. She quickly tossed the photo back into the file and returned the file to her briefcase that was stored under the seat in front of her. This was business, not pleasure. She wasn't on her way to Pepperton looking for love; she was looking for a promotion.

∞

Coach Darren Shaw sat on the edge of his desk giving his ninth grade Algebra class a pep talk about staying safe and enjoying the Thanksgiving holiday. Not only was it the end of the day, but it was the day before school recessed for a holiday, and the students still gave him their full attention. His students respected him and saw him as a role model; so whenever he spoke, he commanded their attention, no matter the time of day. When the bell rang, several of his students stopped to shake his hand on their way out of the door. When the last student left, he vacated his seat on the edge of the wooden desk and walked to his post outside the building for afterschool duty.

"Hey Coach!" Marcus, one of the tenth-grade basketball players, called to Darren, who was walking down the hall toward an exit.

"Hey Marcus, ready for the break?"

"Yes sir! Just wanted to thank you again for helping me with my Algebra. I passed my test."

"You worked hard so I'm not surprised. Congrats man!" Darren added a fist bump before Marcus jogged ahead toward the exit with Darren following behind.

Darren waved off his students as they loaded the buses, heading home for the Thanksgiving break. When the school yard settled down and the buses had all driven away, he walked back to his classroom. After cleaning the dry erase board and putting away a few books that wouldn't be used over the next week, he returned to his seat and pulled out a framed photo of him and Jessica that he kept in his desk. He ran his fingers across the picture of him with his late wife. When she died in a car accident five years ago, so did his dreams of having children and spending treasured holiday time with family.

To keep from feeling sorry for himself, he vowed to spend this time helping the kids that he loved so much. It also gave their parents a break during the recess. He smiled at the picture and whispered *I love you* as he often did. He made it a point not to feel sorry for himself, and he wasn't going to start now. He returned the frame to his drawer, grabbed his backpack and stood to go home. He had some planning to do for his holiday festivities for the kids this year. He also had to get the details to the local paper. They printed a story about it every year. He figured he'd get a jump start on it this year so that he wouldn't have to be bothered while he and the students were concentrating on their projects. He was certain that whoever the *Pepperton Quad* had working on the story this year would be pleased.

∞

Kensi fumbled with her carry-on bags as she walked to claim her luggage. This airport was a small fraction of the size of New York City's airport. From the time she took about five hundred steps from the terminal and turned the corner, she could see the rest of the airport: baggage claim, passenger pick-up and rental car area.

While waiting for the rest of her bags at baggage claim, she took in her surroundings and noticed that she seemed to be the only one in a rush. The other passengers and their families all moved at a much slower speed, taking time for hugs and conversation as if they had nowhere to be. She smiled and figured it must be that easy-going country life that she'd heard so much about.

"You're not from around here, are you?" Kensi turned to find an older white-haired gentleman assessing her.

"No, I'm not," she answered. "How do you know?"

"I've never seen you before," he said and smiled. "Pepperton is about this big." He snapped his fingers. "I run the general store and I've seen everyone in there a time or two. And I've never seen you in church either."

"I'll be here for a while, so I'm sure I'll get a chance to come to both your store and church. Is there really only one church around here?"

"Yep! Nice place with a lot of nice people." When her bags came rolling around on the conveyor, he picked them up and placed them on the floor next to her. "Need help with these?"

"I can handle it. I'm just going to roll them. See?" she popped the handle up.

"Well, anytime you need anything, just stop by the general store," the older gentleman offered, grabbed his duffle bag, tipped his hat and headed toward the passenger pick-up doors. Kensi nodded and went to get her rental car.

After tossing her luggage into the rental, she put the hotel address into her phone's GPS, noticing it wasn't far away. She was quite surprised to see that there were two hotels in town. With a town so small, she wondered why anyone would want to travel here. What would they do?

Pepperton was much prettier than she imagined. The hills were covered in green grass as if it were summer. Only ten minutes away from the airport, she passed a beautiful blue lake where little children and their parents were out feeding ducks. It was warm for a November day. Nothing like the chilly temperatures in New York.

Upon check-in, she concluded that most everyone in the town was friendly. Strangers who were entering and exiting the hotel spoke with her and held open doors. She wasn't exactly used to that anymore, since she'd been living in New York for nearly ten years.

"So what brings you here?" the hotel clerk asked as he went through the process of checking her in. His voice was chipper and welcoming. Hospitality suited him well, Kensi thought.

"Work." She didn't offer any details.

"In Pepperton? Mind if I ask what you do?"

"I'm a journalist for The Big Apple Arts Chronicle in New York. Ever heard of it?"

"I haven't but it sounds fancy. They sent you all the way to Pepperton to do your journaling?"

"Something like that."

"Well, in your free time check out this brochure of our little town. There are lots of great things going on around here for the holidays. Hopefully you'll find everything you need while you're here. Just give us a buzz if you need anything, we'll be more than happy to assist you Ms. Jacobson. Enjoy your stay." With a friendly smile pasted across his face, he handed her the town's brochure along with the room key shaped like the state of Texas.

She was tired from the trip; her plan was to relax for the rest of the day and get started first thing tomorrow. When she entered the room and tossed her luggage into the closet, she plopped across the bed and thumbed through the brochure. There he was again: Mr. Darren Shaw, posing with a group of students. *Is he the town's celebrity?* She wondered. That was the only page she read, telling herself that she was doing research for work. But she had to admit that he was very handsome. His piercing dark eyes and strong jawline were attention grabbing. As much as she didn't want to be in Pepperton, she looked forward to learning what made Mr. Darren Shaw special enough for Samantha to cover his story while she was in Pepperton on her training assignment.

∞

Definitely not what I was expecting, Kensi thought as she pulled into the parking lot of *Pepperton Quad.* She admired her surroundings. The building was about ten stories high with glass windows covering the entire structure. It reminded her of something she'd see in a big city, not what she thought she'd see in a small town like Pepperton. The newspaper's logo with the maroon-colored letters P and Q plastered across a large metal globe was strategically placed on the freshly manicured lawn.

She had an 8:00 appointment and was greeted at the entrance of the building by Sandra Barfield, Executive Vice President of Marketing and Audience Development.

"I'm Kensi Jacobson." Kensi extended her hand.

"Nice to meet you. We've all heard so much about you. Put that hand away, that's nonsense. We are all family here." Miss Sandra gave her a hug. Kensi felt like she was in the presence of a long-lost relative. "Welcome to the Quad," Sandra Barfield greeted Kensi as she led her up from the lobby to the conference room on the seventh floor. The *Pepperton Quad* was affectionately known as the Quad because it covered local stories and events from Pepperton as well as three small surrounding towns: Brandon, Millsville, and Stapleton. None of them was more than fifteen miles outside of Pepperton.

"You'll get started after Thanksgiving, but I wanted to meet you and give you a chance to meet the trainees and ask any questions you may have," Miss Sandra began as she closed the door to the conference room behind her.

Miss Sandra introduced the trainees, Mark, Jennifer, and Tyler, and gave them an opportunity to discuss their background. Kensi managed to muster up a bit of enthusiasm as she talked about her education and career in journalism without mentioning her recent disappointment. Although this wasn't what she would have chosen for herself, she was starting to look forward to sharing her knowledge with the trio.

Miss Sandra dismissed them and they all rose to shake Kensi's hand before exiting the conference room. Kensi smiled and nodded as Miss Sandra took the opportunity to discuss her expectations. Not that she was excited to be there, but Kensi smiled because Miss Sandra's voice reminded her of Blanche's from the eighties television series, *The Golden Girls*.

"Print is no longer working around here, so we'll be transitioning to a digital platform soon. I'll send you an e-mail that contains everything you need to know about our training timetable and your contract details. Do you have any questions for me?"

"It sounds pretty straightforward, so I don't have any questions right now."

Miss Sandra took that as an opportunity to talk more about Pepperton, the Quad, and anything else that came to mind, before taking Kensi around to meet the staff. She was greeted with friendly smiles, handshakes, and even a few hugs. Kensi appreciated the warmth she received, which was quite the opposite of what she had become accustomed to. She felt welcomed and that made it difficult for her to hold on to the grudge she'd been forming for even having to be there in the first place.

"Let me know when you're free for lunch or dinner," Miss Sandra said, as she walked Kensi back to the elevator bank.

"Indeed, I will."

"I know just the place that'll have you falling in love with Pepperton in no time," Miss Sandra continued, flicking her wrist to check the time. "I should be going now. Speaking of food, my husband is probably acting like he's starved since I didn't prepare breakfast for him this morning. I need to make sure he's squared away for lunch. I'll be in touch my dear."

That went well, Kensi thought during her elevator ride back to the ground floor. Part of her was starting to look forward to her time in Pepperton. Maybe, just maybe, it wasn't going to be so bad after all.

CHAPTER 3

Kensi was scheduled to meet with Darren Shaw at 1:30 p.m. After her meeting at *Pepperton Quad*, she spent the rest of the morning reviewing her files and finding out what the internet said about him. Dressed in a featherweight sweater, blue jeans and a pair of flats, she grabbed her crossbody purse, notepad and tape recorder and headed for her rental car.

It seemed that the average time to get anywhere in town took about less than ten minutes. Leaving at one would allow her a few extra minutes to jot some notes when she arrived at the school.

There was only one car in the parking lot when she arrived. She didn't expect many cars because the students were out for their Thanksgiving break. She grabbed her things and started up the concrete path, lined with green bushes and mulch on either side. She hadn't been back to anyone's high school since she graduated, and the front doors of Pepperton High School brought back many memories, decorated with well wishes for the holidays and school announcements.

"You must be Kensi," Darren said, opening the front door when she made it within ten feet of the entrance.

When his principal told him that a journalist would be in town for a while to write the story about their holiday activities, he had no idea that the journalist would look like Kensi. The first thing he noticed were her beautiful almond-shaped eyes half hidden behind her glasses. Her hair, tucked neatly behind her ears, flowed down to the middle of her back. She wore very little makeup, if any at all, except for the tinted lip gloss. Her perfume captivated him as well. It was subtle and fresh, reminding him of powder. He smiled as he held the door open, assessing her.

"Yes, it's a pleasure to meet you, Mr. Shaw."

"Please call me Darren."

Kensi nodded and smiled, noticing that his teeth were even more perfect than they looked in his photo. His eyes were dark but warm and inviting. The photo didn't do him any justice; he could have easily been a model with his strong features.

"So I have to ask. Why not do this at home? It's the holidays," Kensi inquired as she followed him to his classroom. The echo of their voices could be heard in the hallway given the serenity of the atmosphere. Kensi took note of the championship trophies in the glass casing, holiday posters, and the scent that reminded her being inside of a school. They all seemed to have the same smell, at least Pepperton had the same scent of her former high school.

"It's easier for me to focus here. Not many distractions at home, but I guess this is just what I prefer. It's usually filled with students and their chatter, but during vacation times, it's like a sanctuary. I pray over the school, students and teachers while I'm here."

Kensi nodded again, her smile never leaving her face.

Darren led her to his classroom, where he was putting together plans for the holiday event.

"So, is this where the magic happens?" Kensi inquired, glancing around the classroom, but her gaze landed on the papers strewn across his desk.

"I guess you can say that. Have a seat." He gestured toward one of the empty desks. He took a seat next to her instead of sitting at his desk. He clasped his hands together and began, "All right, what do you need from me?"

"Let's start with you. Tell me about Darren Shaw. How did you get started? It seems as if you're the town celebrity, so just tell me all about yourself. Do you mind if I record our conversation?" Kensi asked, pulling out her tape recorder. After getting the okay from Darren, she hit record and placed the contraption on the desk.

She propped her chin on her hands and listened intently, scribbling notes, even though she had the tape recorder running.

Around the time his wife passed away, Darren was offered a coaching position in Pepperton. He'd done a phenomenal job turning around the athletic department of a small school in Houston and became a highly sought-after coach. He loved Houston and probably would have never considered moving but after losing Jessica, there was no way he could stay. Everything in Houston reminded him of her. Their home. Their church. The parks he passed every day to get to work. The grocery stores they shopped in on Sundays.

Having no family in Houston, he saw Pepperton as the perfect opportunity to start over. He didn't want to be reminded that he lost the love of his life. Besides his own heart reminding him, he had to see the looks of pity from his coworkers and church family. He needed time to grieve and it was killing him being fussed over at every turn.

He and Jessica had talked about having kids. In fact, they were trying to get pregnant when she passed away. He had so much love in his heart for children and he didn't want that to die, so he pledged to pour his love into the teenagers of Pepperton High School—those that would receive it.

He had grown fond of the kids and wanted to do more for them and the town of Pepperton. That is when God gave him the idea of the town's Christmas extravaganza, an event geared toward bringing the community together to celebrate the holiday season. He'd been hosting it for the past four years and the town had grown to look forward to it. It was now an annual event, something that he hoped would go on even after he left Pepperton, if he ever did leave.

"Thanksgiving week marked the kick-off for the event. Up until the Tuesday before Thanksgiving, all the students who want to participate have an opportunity to sign up for the activities they want to be part of, whether that's decorating a float for the parade, volunteering at the Christmas tree lighting ceremony, making gifts for parents, or performing in the Christmas theatrical production."

"And you do all of this by yourself?"

"It has actually gotten so big that there is no way that I could pull this off by myself. Some of the other teachers and parents volunteer. This event brings the whole town together. It's so amazing; I've never witnessed anything quite like it." Before Darren moved to Pepperton, the town's Christmas activities were limited to the Christmas parade that took place the Saturday before Christmas.

Kensi agreed, but she wasn't thinking about the event, she was thinking about the host. What an amazing man! A heart for God and children. Too bad she was there for work.

"I'll be tagging along here and there to watch you guys work. I'm not sure if your principal explained that to you. I hope that's okay."

"Not a problem at all. You may just get swept up and help us out a little yourself." Darren winked.

"Hmmm. So do you have a theme?"

"Not really. We've just sort of rolled with the activities, but never a real theme in place. Maybe that's something you could do?"

"Sure, I may be able to help with that."

"Now, since you're going to be hanging around here, I must know who you are besides being a journalist. Tell me about Kensi Jacobson. You've basically gotten my whole life story. Let's hear yours."

Focus, Kensi. This is business. Darren had the most beautiful eyes she'd ever seen. Something about them made her want to stare into them forever. She blinked several times and glanced around his classroom before answering his question. She didn't get too personal, but told him that she was originally from Virginia, where she went to college and how she landed her current position at the *Big Apple Arts Chronicle*.

Darren wanted to know more about her, but for purposes of this project, it wasn't necessary. He figured he would find out enough about her in the coming weeks. It came as a surprise that she intrigued him. He hadn't thought twice about any woman since losing Jessica. Tearing himself away from his personal thoughts, he slid out of the student desk to get his file, including the list of students who signed up to participate in this year's events.

Now that the introductions were out of the way, it was time for him to start contacting the students and allowing Miss Kensi to see the process from start to finish.

CHAPTER 4

Kensi did not want to see another telephone after helping Darren place phone calls to the students who were participating in this year's *Pepperton Christmas*. She had thought it would only take about an hour, but it took several hours to accomplish. From questions from parents to some students wanting to chat about how excited they were to take part in the event, she imagined that it must have been near dusk when they finished.

"Fun stuff, right?" Darren grinned after placing the last call.

"Busy work is more like it, but they all seemed pretty excited." A smile spread across Kensi's face as she thought of the joy that Darren was bringing into their lives.

"So does that mean you're going to join me tomorrow? I could really use the help; it's not like I have my team together yet. Maybe you could help me get things sorted out."

"Umm, sure, I don't mind." Kensi didn't have anything else to do, and being hands-on would allow her to develop her story.

Darren enjoyed her company and wanted to see her sooner rather than later. He could have handled everything by himself, but since the event seemed to be getting bigger and bigger, having an extra pair of hands around couldn't hurt. The fact that the owner of those hands was one of the most beautiful women he'd laid eyes on in a long time didn't hurt either.

Darren stood to walk Kensi out of the school. He was a little unsure of himself, and waited with his hands tucked in both pockets. He hadn't asked a woman out since his wife died, so he wasn't sure he even knew how to do it anymore.

"Say, I know I've kept you here probably longer than you expected. Would you like to grab a bite to eat? Seeing as much of our town as possible could help with your story, I'm sure," he added to appear more casual. He watched her as she gathered her portfolio and tape recorder. She was graceful about everything she did. He couldn't help noticing all the little things about her. He was lonely for lack of companionship all these years, and he wondered if she was as well put together as she seemed.

"Food sounds really good right about now." She had been planning to dine alone in a local eatery about a block away from her hotel but she enjoyed his company. Besides, it would give her another opportunity to see why this town found him so fascinating.

Darren extended his hand toward the door with a slight nod of his head as Kensi strode past him toward the door. To stave off the awkward silence during their walk to the parking lot, Darren talked about plans for the next day—how the students would be separated by age and interest before the assignments were given and how he needed Kensi to assist.

When they reached the parking lot, Darren opened Kensi's door to help her inside. When she was safely inside and buckled up, he gave her a rundown of the route, although she would be following him. He walked the short distance to his car. When he started his car and pulled away, he exhaled, and realized that he'd been holding his breath. He smiled at the thought of Kensi. He was grateful that they met under these circumstances, because he wasn't sure how he would have reacted otherwise.

Some of his colleagues and church members had tried to set him up with what they thought was the perfect mate. He was past being set up at this point in this life. He didn't think he could ever be with another woman after Jessica, but something about Kensi made him think twice about that.

Darren took a different route than the one Kensi used to get to Pepperton High. As she drove behind him, she admired the beautiful live oak trees, thinking that they were much too green for this time of the year. She saw signage that read "Come one, Come all! Join us for Thanksgiving service and dinner." That was new to her. She had never seen anything like that in New York. But then again, New York City was a thousand times larger than Pepperton. There was no way everyone could be fed.

Millers Smokehouse. Kensi eyeballed the plain display stationed in front of a wooden building. She could smell what she recognized as mesquite smoke the moment she opened her car door. The scent of the barbecue tantalized her nostrils, making her stomach rumble.

"I hope this is as delicious as it smells," Kensi said to Darren as he walked over to her car door, extending his hand to help her out of the car.

"Oh yeah! I'm sure it's better than any barbecue you've ever had in your entire life."

"Life, huh?"

"Trust me on this. This is pat-your-belly-give-me-seconds-thirds-and-fourths kind of good." Darren laughed as he led her to the entrance, holding the door open for her to enter first.

"Sounds like you work for them. Is this your second job?"

Darren chuckled at her assessment. "No, I just know good food, that's all.

"So what do you usually order?" Kensi stood in front of an easel reading the menu that had been written in chalk.

"Sausage baked potato and a half rack of baby back ribs."

Kensi nodded and curled her lips into a slight smile before turning her attention back to the hand-written menu. She decided on a pulled chicken baked potato and strawberry lemonade. After placing their orders, grabbing a number and finding seats, Darren opened the conversation again, asking more about Kensi's background and why she decided to become a journalist.

Kensi loved that question and delved into the details behind her decision, explaining how she had always loved to read and write. She wanted to write stories that people wanted to read, but she also wanted to make a living while doing it. Becoming a novelist wasn't enough for her—she didn't have the patience to wait until her books got into the right hands to gain enough success to make a living while doing it. Although one day she planned to write a few books, now wasn't the time. She enjoyed being part of the story and interviewing those whom she wrote about. Now more than any time in the past, she was getting to do that, even though she was nearly a thousand miles away from home.

This wasn't the way she imagined it, but she convinced herself that she wasn't being punished for not getting the promotion and that getting to come to Pepperton was what she needed and what she enjoyed.

She could go on and on about the joy and purpose she found in her work, but she was interrupted when their food arrived. She excused herself and bowed her head to say a prayer of thanks for her food. When she finished, she noticed Darren staring at her with a smirk on his face.

"You know . . . around here, we all pray together. We're a family so it's rude to sit at a table with other people and pray without including them. At least that's the rule around here. My rule. I'll let you slide this time, but take note of that for the future," Darren teased before saying a quick prayer himself.

"Noted." Kensi saluted and dipped her fork into the baked potato loaded with smoked pulled chicken, shredded cheese, sour cream and a touch of butter, salt and pepper. She closed her eyes as the food melted in her mouth. She wasn't sure if it was as great as Darren described earlier or if she was just nearly starving, but she had to admit it was delicious.

Darren watched her a moment before starting. "See, what did I tell you? It's the bomb huh? Tell me you can get that in New York."

"I'm not sure if I can, I just know I never have. This is so good," Kensi answered before taking another bite.

There was not a lot of chatter between the two of them after their food had arrived. Kensi couldn't stop eating, amazed at how tasty the baked potato was. The two of them stole a few glances at the other from time to time but didn't say a lot. They simply enjoyed each other's company, not wanting to leave even after dinner was over.

"I'm gonna have to make it out here at least once a week until I leave. I'm stuffed, but that was the best baked potato I've ever had." Kensi patted her flat stomach.

"This isn't the only great place around here. There is so much more to see in this quaint little town. We can go somewhere else tomorrow if you're up to it after we get the students squared away."

"Sounds good to me."

Darren offered to pay for her meal but she refused. Since she was there for business, her company was taking care of it. However, she took note of him wanting to clear the tab. He was a gentleman at least, she mentally checked off the list, one reason why the town adored him.

CHAPTER 5

Darren was just as amazed as anyone else at how important *A Pepperton Christmas* had come to be. The town enjoyed the first event so much so that the citizens voted in favor of city funding to make it an annual event; that way Darren would have everything he needed to host *A Pepperton Christmas* and the students would have something constructive to keep them busy. Everyone in town anticipated the heartwarming parade, the festival of lights, and the lighting of the town's Christmas tree coupled with the snow festival.

Darren went to the local Wal-Mart to start gathering craft supplies to decorate the floats for the parade, lights and ornaments for the Christmas tree, and a few items that he thought would prove beneficial in the construction of the handmade gifts for the parents. Each year participation multiplied, so he wanted to get a head start on the shopping. Although he didn't mind this part of the task, he was starting to think that the trip would have been a lot more fun if Kensi were there with him. For some reason, her opinion mattered to him.

He didn't know much about her yet, but was enjoying getting to know her. She was the first woman that he'd spent time with since Jessica. When everyone else in town tried to set him up with a woman, he compared the woman to Jessica or gave the excuse that he wasn't ready yet. Though a part of him would always love and miss her, he would move on if he found the right woman. He loved what he did for those kids in Pepperton, but he'd be lying to himself if he said he didn't want to have children of his own to create special traditions and memories with.

He'd been standing in the same spot for the last ten minutes, holding two boxes of lights. His intention was to compare the two to see if one brand would be better than the brand they'd used in prior years, but the thoughts swirling around in his mind took his mind off the task.

"Darren!"

Darren's head snapped around when he heard a woman calling his name from the opposite end of the aisle, drawing him back into the present. He hoped it was Kensi, but that would have been too good to be true. He squinted, trying to make out who she was. Neither the long, crinkled hair nor the baby she had in tow helped ring a bell. He tried to place her voice, but that didn't help. And nothing about her slender frame jolted any recognition. She didn't move from her position, only waved enthusiastically with one hand while holding on to a shopping cart with the other.

"Hey!" he spoke and smiled.

"Getting ready for the town's Christmas festivities?" the woman asked, determined to have a conversation from about fifty feet away. Still, Darren had no clue who she was, so he pushed his cart to the end of the aisle, hoping to remember her name. He hated when someone recalled his name but he couldn't do the same.

"I am. The cart gave me away, huh? Are you going to be able to make it this year?" he asked, thinking that if she spoke long enough, he would recall whether he knew her from church or someplace else. Even though they lived in a small town, he couldn't remember everyone.

"You know I wouldn't miss it. I have to take this little one to see it," she cooed, her voice changing to include the baby in the conversation. "Isn't that right, sweetheart?"

"How's your husband?"

"Oh, Nate is fine!" she answered with a wave of her hand.

That is how he knew her. She was the wife of one of his colleagues. He quickly searched his memory for her name. Shelly. That had to be it.

"Shelly, right? It was good seeing you. I need to take off and finish shopping."

"Good seeing you, too. Next time, bring along some help. Maybe the journalist lady," she tossed over her shoulder as she pushed the cart away.

Nothing in this town was a secret. He should have known that the town would be talking after he had dinner with Kensi yesterday. Since he'd never been out with anyone, they'd likely assume that he liked her, never mind that she was there on business. All they saw was a man and a woman who had obviously taken a liking to each other. Shelly was dabbling into his personal life, but he had to agree with her. That shopping trip would have been much more fun if Kensi had come along to join him.

Wrapping up his purchases, he found himself wondering whether or not Kensi would like certain colors, fabrics or decorations more than he thought about the children's taste. After checking out and loading his car, he decided that next time he would just ask her to come along. She was there on assignment, after all, and the more she was part of the process, the more information she would have to complete her articles. That way, they would both be getting what they wanted—more for her story and more time with him.

Chapter 6

Kensi's lips curled into a scowl at the name glowing on her vibrating cell phone screen. Her boss. Ugh. After everything that happened the last time she saw Samantha, she was still pretty sour, though she tried hard to deny it and tried even harder to stave off those feelings by repeating Scripture every time any ill thought popped into her mind about the ordeal. She didn't want to harbor any resentment, but she was failing at keeping it away. Passing over her was wrong on so many levels. In Kensi's mind, Samantha's best interests were far from her mind; her only concern was making sure her grandson, Adam, kept a job, no matter how terrible he was at it.

Kensi toyed with the idea of letting the phone go to voicemail, but she was on assignment, after all. Maybe that was the call telling her that she'd made a big mistake by promoting Adam over Kensi and that Kensi should jump on the next crop-duster out of Pepperton.

"This is Kensi," she answered the phone more formally than normal.

"How's it going out there?" Kensi could hear the smile in Samantha's voice and that made her back itch. She closed her eyes and took a deep breath. She had to check herself before her attitude reflected in her tone.

"About as good as it could be going," Kensi answered and silently added, *considering I'm in the middle of nowhere.*

"Apparently it's going better than that. I've already received a call from the *Pepperton Quad.* They're trying to steal you away from me. Don't tell me you've decided to leave all of us and stay in Texas!"

She had to be kidding. Kensi wasn't sure if she should even dignify her with a response. What would make her think that? Who would be enjoying themselves out here? She enjoyed the city life, hence the reason she moved to Manhattan in the first place. If she wanted to live in the country, she would have gone back home after college graduation many moons ago.

"I'm not so sure about that," Kensi played along. She wondered what Mrs. Elkins was up to. Was she trying to send her to Timbuktu next?

"I know you'll do well, Kensi, and the right opportunity will send you right where you need to be. You need not worry, my dear."

Where is this coming from? And what is the purpose of this call? Is she trying to feel me out? If so, I'm still pretty pissed about the promotion situation.

Kensi removed the phone from her ear and took a deep breath. She could feel her attitude rising, and if nothing else, she wanted to remain professional. "Thanks."

"I'll have Cedric set up a meeting with you after Thanksgiving to see what you have so far. Let's see if we can warm up the hearts of these New Yorkers for the holidays, shall we?"

"Sounds good."

Kensi sat on the edge of the bed staring at the phone after the call ended. That was weird. Samantha wasn't one to chit-chat without a purpose. Why did she really call? The one thing she'd said that intrigued Kensi was that the local paper had eyes on her. Was that true? Kensi thought about checking into it. Maybe she could use their offer as a bargaining chip to get Samantha to at least compensate her for choosing her grandson over her for the promotion. But who was she kidding? Would Pepperton even be able to afford her?

∞

Thanksgiving in Houston visiting the McKinneys was the perfect solution for sweeping her career issues to the back of her mind. She hadn't seen Raegan since the wedding and was dying to get a chance to spoil the twins.

Kensi's drive into Houston on the eve of Thanksgiving was exactly what she needed. It was late evening, so the town greeted her with heavy traffic and skyscrapers that lit up the night. She took a detour and drove through downtown Houston because it reminded her a little of New York—that was what she enjoyed— the fast life, the hustle and bustle.

But she couldn't pass through without stopping. She pulled over, paid for parking and walked into Itz Coffee. She smiled as she took her place in the order line. It almost felt like home. The only thing missing were patrons with heavy coats and scarves wrapped around their necks, whether it was for fashion or to keep warm.

After the barista made her caramel latte to order, she took a seat near the corner window. Her thoughts swirled as the warm liquid warmed her body. She wondered what kinds of openings were available at the newspaper back in Pepperton. It wasn't that she wanted to move to the little town, but curiosity got the best of her. She whipped out her phone and opened their website.

She sipped and swiped until she came across a position for someone to manage the paper's media presence. *Hmmm. Really?* Her qualifications matched the description perfectly. In fact, her credentials exceeded what they were asking for. However, they were only looking for someone to fill the position temporarily. She had a little extra time on her hands, and it wasn't like she was planning to live in Pepperton permanently. Neither her training duties nor working on the articles would interfere and that position would give her résumé a boost for the moment when she was ready to leave Samantha, who didn't seem to appreciate her anyway.

Kensi spent a few minutes people watching and contemplating whether or not to apply for the position. She loved sitting in coffee shops. A dose of caffeine and watching people who seemed to be content inspired her to seek clarity on her next steps, whatever that tended to be in that moment. This moment was about her career. She thought she had it all planned out, but life handed her another detour. According to her plan, she should have been sitting in New York in the office next to Samantha helping her run the paper. *Well on her way* is how she would have described it, but now it felt like she was moving backward instead of forward.

It couldn't hurt to see what would happen, she thought as she finished off her latte and swiped and tapped until her application was complete. When she moved to leave, she locked eyes and smiles with a few strangers on her way out the door; it was as if they too could sense that she'd taken a step in the right direction.

It also wouldn't hurt that she could possibly get a chance to see a little more of Darren Shaw.

Chapter 7

Raegan flung open the door at the sound of Kensi ringing the doorbell and pulled her into a tight squeeze. She hadn't laid eyes on Kensi since her wedding.

"Oh my gosh, I've missed you so much girlfriend! You look great!" Raegan exclaimed, releasing her embrace to give Kensi a once over.

"Me? Honey, you are the one who looks amazing! I would never have guessed that you gave birth to twins!"

"Now that is a compliment, because it certainly feels like I did," Raegan said and giggled, squeezing the extra skin around her midsection.

Kensi waved off her comment, walked into the house, and searched the area for the babies. The home screamed Thanksgiving, from the autumn blessings décor that hung on the walls and the centerpieces that adorned the end tables to the smell of apple pies and stuffed turkey. There was no doubt that Raegan was getting a jumpstart on their Thanksgiving meal.

"Now you know you should have answered the door with those babies. Where are they?" Kensi half-demanded. She stood in the center of the living room with her arms folded across her chest, with mock impatience.

Raegan chuckled and called to Caleb to bring the kids downstairs to visit with Kensi for a while.

"You do know that it's late and it's near bedtime, right?"

Kensi moved to the end of the stairs with her neck strained waiting for Caleb to descend with the babies. "What are they, like seven months old or something? They're too young to have a bedtime."

"No, silly. They are five months old and it's never too early to start trying to implement good sleeping habits."

"Really Rae?"

"I didn't say that it works, I only said it's never too early to start—"

"Oh my gosh! They are so adorable!" Kensi said, cutting Raegan off when Caleb entered the room with the babies and Nicholas trailing behind him. Raegan took one of them out of his arms and Kensi reached for the other. "They are even more adorable than they look in the pictures."

Kensi's heart swelled with happiness for her friend and the life that she was building with Caleb. She too wanted a happy family, and everyone else around her seemed to be getting it. Things with Adam were going okay and they could have possibly had something together eventually, but that was before he stabbed her in the back.

She then thought about Darren. He could be a good candidate, but he lived in Pepperton. There was no way she would be living there forever and he sure didn't seem like a city guy, so she was left at square one, it seemed, in just about every area of her life.

"Would you like some dinner?" Caleb offered. "We have a few pieces of baked chicken, mashed potatoes and broccoli."

"Depends on who cooked it," Kensi joked. "Was it you? I'm already far from home; I'm not trying to die out here too."

"Yep," Caleb touted proudly.

Kensi looked to Raegan, who ignored the banter between the two.

"Well since Rae here is still alive and is showing no signs of illness, I'll have some."

"C'mon Nicholas, let's fix Auntie Kensi a special plate," Caleb said and chuckled, returning to the kitchen with Nicholas to dish up a late dinner for Kensi. Nicholas happily hopped, kicked and jumped, following Caleb into the kitchen.

Kensi and Raegan sat together while Kensi cooed and played with the twins. In her mind, Raegan had everything—career, husband and family. Tammy had reconciled with Joshua, and even Michelle seemed to be happy with her career change. She wasn't jealous; in fact, she celebrated their happiness, but she wondered when it was going to be her turn.

She grew up dreaming about when she would get married and have kids, but it didn't seem to be in the stars for her. She'd often thought about trying to reconnect with her college love since it seemed to have worked for Raegan, but she'd never forget her father's words, "Never go backwards. If it didn't work then, it won't work now." After all, they broke up on a technicality—long distance. Who's to say that it would be different this time? That is why she would keep her distance from Darren. Long-distance relationships never seemed to work out and that is exactly what would happen if she and Darren decided to give it a shot. There was no way she would spend the rest of her life in a small town and she wouldn't dare allow him to follow her to New York, especially when he seemed to have purpose in Pepperton.

Raegan eyed Kensi carefully. She seemed to be pretty content with a baby in her arms.

"Tell me . . . what's going on with you? Pepperton? Is that even a real town? What is that about?"

"They railroaded me, that's what it's about," Kensi answered. Caleb returned and she exchanged the baby for the plate as she made herself comfortable on the sofa. "You should stay, Caleb. You may be able to offer some good advice, too," Kensi said to a retreating Caleb. He took a seat in the recliner to listen to Kensi's story. He didn't want to be caught up in girl talk, but would stay to offer advice since Kensi invited him.

Kensi prayed silently before starting her dinner. In between bites, she shared what happened back in New York and how she ended up on an assignment in Texas.

"Maybe God is leading you in a different direction? Or maybe there is something else you need to learn before you take that job? Maybe that isn't the job for you," Caleb offered when Kensi finished. "I know sometimes the route we have to take may not be in alignment with the route we think is best, but I believe that everything will work out well for you in the end . . . probably in a much better way than you would have even imagined. Look at me, for example. If anyone had told me three years ago that this would be my life, I would have laughed in their face. You of all people should know that God has a way of working things out," Caleb said before taking a sip of water.

48

"I think he summed it up nicely. That's my baby!" Raegan complimented and blew a kiss in Caleb's direction.

Kensi reluctantly agreed. She knew that Caleb was right, but it didn't feel that way now. She wished that she knew what God's plan was, because she had thought that this was it. She took the career path that suited her well. She didn't choose it because it paid the most money, was glamorous, or it was something that her parents wanted her to do. She'd prayed and the job just fell into place for her. She only wished that she knew why things weren't working out the way they were supposed to right now.

"I won't charge you for my services this time," Caleb teased as he rose to his feet. He left the room with all three children in tow to get them ready for bed.

"I'm sure I couldn't afford you anyway," Kensi tossed over her shoulder.

"Got that right!" Caleb had made it to the top of the stairs but his voice could still be heard over Nicholas' laughter and cries from one of the twins.

Raegan took Kensi's plate to the kitchen and returned to the seat next to her on the couch.

"Caleb is gone now, so what else is going on?" Raegan made herself comfortable, placing one foot under her and resting her elbow against the back of the couch.

Kensi exhaled and pulled her lips into a tight line.

"Not getting the promotion has me assessing everything else in my life. What is really going on? I'm in my thirties. I just thought I'd have everything you guys have at this point in my life. We were all supposed to have this, but now it seems that I'm the only one who doesn't. What's wrong with me?"

Raegan reached out and rubbed Kensi's arm. She thought for a moment before answering. Surely there was nothing wrong with Kensi, but Kensi of all people had to know that God's timing is much different than ours. They were each other's accountability partners before she married Caleb, so Kensi was the one constantly reminding Raegan to trust and wait on God for whatever He had in store for her.

"You're the perfect package. You'll get what you need in time. I believe that, and you need to believe that, too."

"It's not that I don't believe it; it just seems like it's taking forever. This womb won't be able to bear children if I have to wait much longer."

"Have we forgotten Sarah?"

Kensi laughed at the comment. Everyone knew the story of Sarah and she could find encouragement in the fact that God could give her children even if she waited. She just didn't want to be as old as Sarah was.

"Come here, honey. Everything is going to be okay. I just know it will," Raegan said and pulled Kensi into her arms. "Wanna pray about it? 'Cause you know that the Word of the Lord says that when two or three are gathered together in His name—"

"There He is in the midst of them," Kensi quoted the Scripture along with Raegan before they prayed. Kensi felt a little better after praying with Raegan. Although she'd been praying about the situation alone, there was something empowering about having someone praying in agreement with her. For a moment, she was glad that her assignment sent her to Pepperton; she would be able to spend the holiday with her best friend and maybe get a new perspective on life.

"Now come on and take some of that frustration out on these veggies. I could use a little help chopping," Raegan insisted and pulled Kensi up from the couch to help. With the knife in her hand, Kensi thought about all that had been happening in her life, and chopped the onions, pepper and celery as if it were their fault. Maybe this was the start of everything she needed. Or so she hoped.

Chapter 8

Kensi turned her eyes away from the Macy's Thanksgiving Day parade to check her vibrating cell phone. Her head began pounding at the number displayed on the caller ID. Although she'd deleted Adam's number, she'd seen it displayed across her screen enough to recognize it without his name attached to it. She chewed her bottom lip and thought for a moment. Should she answer it? Was he calling to apologize again or to deliver news that he'd decided to pass on the promotion so that she could get what she rightfully deserved?

She swiped the green phone on the touch screen. "Hello."

She excused herself from the family room and walked through the French doors to the patio to speak privately. If the conversation turned sour, she wanted to speak freely, and she couldn't do that with little Nicholas sitting within earshot.

"How've you been?" Adam asked hesitantly to feel her out. He hated the way their last encounter ended. If he never saw or spoke to her again, he didn't want that to be her last memory of him. He wasn't as bad as she thought he was. He planned to tell her about the promotion; he just hadn't had the chance.

"Good, actually. You?"

"I'm making it. Trying not to freeze to death. What is the weather like out there?"

Kensi paced back and forth on the patio. She wasn't in the mood for small talk today, so she kept her response brief and prayed that Adam called with a purpose. "Fine. About 70 degrees today."

"That sounds nice. . . . Listen, I just want to apologize again about how things went down. I hope you know that you're still amazing at what you do, and this job has no bearing on it."

"Hmm," Kensi said and rolled her eyes heavenward. She wasn't sure what he expected her to say to that. She knew how great she was and how he wasn't half as good as her, but that didn't seem to matter.

"You know I couldn't have turned it down even if I wanted to. It would break her heart, you know? She's been waiting on the moment when she could turn the reins over to me and retire."

"I see." Kensi continued pacing back and forth on the patio, wondering why Adam felt the need to defend his grandmother's decision. It was her decision to make. The only person who needed to back it was her.

Adam sighed loudly into the receiver. He knew it was a mistake calling her. He was probably making the situation worse and not encouraging her the way he wanted to do.

"So are you still intent on ending things between us because of this?"

"Well, weren't you intent on keeping your little promotion a secret?"

"You know that's not true, Kens! Stop making this about us. Our careers have nothing to do with our relationship, and you know that. You just needed an out and this was the perfect opportunity for you."

"No! Adam, how am I supposed to trust you? You let me walk right into that office thinking that I was about to get the job. You could have said something . . . anything. You had plenty of opportunity to tell me the truth, but instead you hid behind your granny! I suspect that you'll always be hiding behind her or something else. If I can't trust you, I can't be with you. Simple as that!" Kensi retorted, not realizing that her voice was elevated to the point where she grabbed the attention of the family inside the house.

"Fine, whatever. Happy Thanksgiving."

"Yea, same to you. Good-bye Adam," Kensi said with finality, ending the call. She took a deep breath and entered the house to find Caleb, Raegan and Nicholas' eyes locked on her.

"Are you all right Auntie Kensi?" Nicholas asked, sounding as if he had a handful of grapes in his mouth. He was clearly concerned and confused after witnessing her yelling into the phone, something he wasn't accustomed to seeing. From the other side of the glass, she looked like a madwoman pacing back and forth with flailing arms.

"Yes, baby, I'm fine."

Raegan and Caleb looked one to another and then to Kensi, who shrugged her shoulders and smiled.

"Really, I'm good. No worries."

Kensi didn't say anything else about it and neither did they.

∞

One of the things Adam admired about Kensi was her ambition, but to allow a promotion to drive a wedge between them was a bit extreme. Upset and driven by his emotional conversation with Kensi, he marched into his grandmother's office in hopes of finding a solution, one where he and Kensi could both get what they wanted. They hadn't been seeing each other long, but he felt like their relationship had potential to become something special. If he couldn't find a way to make this right, then it certainly would be over for good.

"Gigi, do you realize what you've done?" he questioned Samantha, closing the door behind him. He didn't usually address her at work that way, but his work life became personal when she passed over Kensi for assistant editor-in-chief.

Samantha flipped her silver strands over her shoulder, folded her arms, rested her back against the chair and raised one perfectly arched eyebrow. She didn't say anything, but everything about her persona warned him to tread carefully.

Adam moved from his position at the door and took the seat across from her desk. "Please don't look at me that way, Gigi. I told you this would happen."

"What exactly do you mean?"

"You know how hard Kensi has worked and how badly she wanted to fill your shoes. She's your protégé for goodness sake! You've trained her for this," he answered, gesturing toward her desk.

"This is business. Miss Jacobson understands this and so should you. When I'm done, someone has to run this place." Samantha had other reasons for not giving Kensi the position that she rightfully earned. She adored and respected Kensi, but she needed Kensi to spread her wings and fly. Kensi had the potential to be so much greater. Samantha couldn't offer her what she needed; she was doing her best to try to keep her business afloat, with digital media taking over. While she appreciated all that technology had improved, she wasn't ready to go that route yet. She still believed there was a need for her paper and that her subscribers enjoyed reading about her coverage of inspiring arts in print, based on their continued subscription.

"And Kensi can't do that?"

"Like I said, this is business – a family business. And the only person who will run it when I leave is you! Haven't I made myself clear?"

Adam leaned forward, his forearm now resting on the desk. "You do know that she wants nothing else to do with me, right? Is this what you wanted? Her out of my life? Is this business of yours more important than my personal life?"

"What is it worth to you? What do you want?" Samantha became agitated. Should changes need to be made with upgrading their platform, she wanted Adam around to do it. She hated to use her position as his grandmother to influence his decision, but she had no choice. He had no commitment with Kensi, so she knew he wouldn't choose her over his family.

"Are you asking me to choose? I just don't see how anyone wins that way. There has to be a way to work this all out."

"Kensi is where she needs to be. She is a distraction to you and it seems you can't focus like you need to when she's around,"

Samantha interrupted. "I won't hear any more of this. I've done what is best and I stand by my decision. Now you make your decision. What's it going to be, Son?"

Adam stood abruptly and shoved his balled fists into his pockets. His piercing blue eyes pleaded with her to find a different way. For all he knew, Kensi could be looking for a new job right now. She was absolutely amazing in her profession; there was no way that she wouldn't be hired if she looked elsewhere. That is what he feared—she would leave and he would never get a chance to work himself back into her good graces.

Chapter 9

The familiar scents of lavender and vanilla welcomed Kensi when she arrived back to her Pepperton hotel room. Glancing toward the bed, the flashing light on the phone immediately caught her attention. *Who would be leaving messages for me at the hotel?* she thought to herself as pushed off her flats with either foot, tossed her duffle bag into the closet and went to check the messages.

She smiled when she heard Darren's voice on the other end of the line. Since the fight she recently had with Adam lingered in the back of her mind, she could use the refreshing. It didn't matter what he was calling about, she found herself glad just because he called. For a moment, she nearly forgot the reason she was in Pepperton. She was there on assignment and not to make a love connection. Darren's message reminded her about the volunteer meeting happening that evening. That would be an opportunity for her to ask questions of the volunteers to get a different take on the event and help with her article.

She made herself comfortable on the bed. She had at least two hours before the meeting that evening, and since it seemed to take less than ten minutes to drive from any point in town to the other, she had plenty of time to relax. She could get to the meeting in a jiffy.

She turned on her phone to check e-mails. After her argument with Adam, she turned her phone off for the rest of the weekend, only turning it on to call her parents to wish them a Happy Thanksgiving. She had received an e-mail from the local paper in response to her job application. With a response that quick, she immediately assumed it was a rejection and decided to open it later. Seeing nothing else important, she set her alarm and settled into bed for a nap.

∞

"It is really nice to see you again, Kensi," Darren said, holding her gaze while his right hand engulfed hers with a slow handshake. That was quite different from what he instinctively wanted to do, but seemed most appropriate given the fact that they were surrounded by the town's volunteers and he didn't want to make her uncomfortable by pulling her into his arms for a hug.

"Same here," Kensi responded. They didn't release hands, instead, Darren escorted her just inside of the auditorium where everyone else was gathered.

He briefed her on the agenda, handing her a tablet with details on the meeting, as he guided her to a seat at the end of the front row.

"We will proceed as usual, but feel free to stop us at any moment for clarity. The environment is casual; we won't mind if you interrupt us. We're all friends here. We'd be happy to help you get everything you need to highlight our little ole town for the big city folk," he said to her as she took her seat, flashing his bright white smile.

"Thanks. You do know you don't have to do that with your voice, right?"

"What's wrong with my voice?"

"You had this country twang going on a minute ago. Unnecessary. I can very well tell you're from around here without you having to do all of that," Kensi teased.

Darren chuckled softly before walking away to start the meeting. He opened with a few words of prayer and proceeded with the meeting following the agenda that he'd given out. Kensi took notes, updating them here and there with as much information as possible. Samantha wanted a story and that was exactly what she was going to get. Kensi would make her sorry for ever passing her up for Adam.

When Darren wrapped up the meeting, a few hands flew into the air for the question and answer session.

"Have we decided on attire yet?" Mrs. Caldwell asked. She joined the meeting about twenty minutes late and didn't see any mention of it on the agenda.

"Not yet. Would you like to help us out and oversee that?"

"Sure. I don't mind." Mrs. Caldwell sat on the edge of her seat with her glasses on the brim of her nose, ecstatic once again that the costumes would be her contribution to the Christmas festivities, not that anyone else would be up for it anyway since Mrs. Caldwell was the town's seamstress. She particularly specialized in wedding and formal attire, but took pride in overseeing the holiday costumes.

"Anyone else?" Darren asked, waving his hand in front of the podium.

Three more parents asked questions about someone overseeing the float decorations, managing the volunteers at the tree lighting festival, and snacks for the students during rehearsals. Any other questions were missed by Kensi when Miss Sandra came over to speak with her.

"Did you get everything you needed, my dear?" Miss Sandra asked Kensi while the meeting was wrapping up, interrupting her train of thought as she jotted down her final notes.

"Yes ma'am, I did."

"Oh, don't call me ma'am. That only reminds me of how old I really am. I'd like to think that I'm still young," Miss Sandra said, sitting down next to Kensi. "So what is this all about? I doubt many people ever even heard of Pepperton. Why here? Why this?" She gestured with the wave of her hand. Though it was a nice event, Miss Sandra figured that Samantha must have been trying to find busy work for Kensi aside from her training duties.

I've been asking myself the same question, Kensi thought and smiled. "The boss wants what the boss wants. This is sort of a special assignment," she answered.

"Well, this is a special place and I imagine you've come to know that for yourself by now. I've been here twenty years and I couldn't see myself anywhere else. If you ever need anything while you're here, just give me a call. I mean it," Miss Sandra reminded her, just as she did when they'd met a week ago.

Seeing Miss Sandra reminded Kensi of her application for the temporary position at the newspaper. Coincidence? Kensi didn't believe in those. Maybe there was a reason for her seeing Miss Sandra today, given she hadn't seen her since the day they met at *Pepperton Quad*'s offices. She could talk to her about

Pepperton Quad and see if that was something she really wanted to pursue, pending the content in the e-mail. Whatever the case, she had a feeling that things were turning around and God was up to something. She was ready for whatever came next—no matter where it was going to lead.

"Hey, is everything all right over here? Did this help you at all?" Darren asked as he took the seat next to Kensi that Miss Sandra had just vacated.

"I believe so. I'm looking forward to seeing how this turns out. I mean I've been to these kinds of events before, but I must see why it's such a big deal. No offense to you."

"None taken." Darren paused and looked from Kensi to Miss Sandra's retreating back. "So I see you've met Miss Sandra?"

"This is the second time, but yes, I like her. She seems to be very friendly."

"That she is," Darren said and eyed Kensi carefully.

"What?" Kensi asked. "Why are you being weird all of a sudden?" His thoughtful stare didn't make her uncomfortable, but she was starting to grow concerned.

"I just had a funny thought."

"And what was that exactly?"

Darren contemplated whether or not he would share it with her. Seeing her talking with Miss Sandra and knowing what they both did for a living, he couldn't help but wonder if they were talking about a job opportunity. Seeing how much Kensi enjoyed the city life and pretty much wanted to get this project behind her as soon as possible, he was certain working in Pepperton was the last thing on her mind.

He decided to test his theory. "Miss Sandra trying to recruit you for the local paper. Everyone around here knows how good you are. Small town. People talk. That should be one thing you've learned since you've been here."

"I doubt she was trying to recruit me," Kensi answered and added silently, *probably wanting to explain why they had to say no.* She immediately chastised herself for that thought, seeing as though she hadn't read her e-mails. It was best that she held off on that until she was locked in her hotel room for the rest of the night. She'd much rather deal with the outcome in her personal space. Yes or no, she'd have to deal with how to proceed, although another rejection was not what she needed right now.

Darren reserved his comments and stood up from his seat, extending his hand to help Kensi out of hers. Carrying her things for her, he accompanied her back to her rental car.

"Hey . . . I am here to help with whatever you need. I'm only a phone call away."

"I won't forget it," Kensi replied before closing the door. When she was safely inside, buckled up and engine on, he tapped the roof of the car and stepped aside to watch her back away. When her tail lights faded in the distance, he walked back inside the auditorium to grab his things. Everyone had left and once again, he was alone with his thoughts. He pulled out his cell phone to replay an old voicemail from Jessica, but thought against it. That is what he usually did when he got lonely, but tonight he felt guilty because the voice he wanted to hear had just backed out of the parking lot heading back to her hotel room.

Chapter 10

A large lump formed in Kensi's throat as she read and re-read the e-mail in response to her application. They wanted her. At least they wanted her to come in for an interview. She responded to the e-mail indicating that she would be available for the date and time suggested. She closed the apps on her phone and set it on the nightstand next to the bed. Darren's words played through her mind. *Small town. People talk.*

Did he know? Did Miss Sandra know already? She pulled the Bible from the top drawer in the nightstand and flipped it open. She didn't have any particular Scripture in mind; all she knew was that she needed a word of encouragement and there was no better place to turn.

She closed her eyes and said a quick prayer. When she looked down at the open Bible in her lap, her eyes gravitated toward Jeremiah 29:11, "For I know the thoughts that I think toward you, says the Lord, thoughts of peace and not of evil, to give you a future and a hope."

Tears rolled down her cheeks as she read and re-read the Scripture. She took out a pen and pad from the hotel nightstand and read the Scripture in context, jotted down notes, read the commentary, and prayed. She even revisited some old notes she had in her phone from a sermon where Jeremiah 29:11 was the focal Scripture. She'd read it a hundred times before and even had it memorized, but in that moment, it meant a whole lot more than it ever did. She was practically alone in a strange place with her life turned upside down, not knowing what her next move would be, but now she had a little more faith to trust in God. Although she had her own plans and thoughts of where she should be at this point in her life, she wasn't quite sure what God was up to and how things were going to work out. She was just certain that they would.

∞

"Good afternoon. I love your dress," Miss Sandra complimented Kensi upon greeting her at the restaurant's entrance. Her voice was bright, country and cheery, just like Kensi remembered. They met at Pepperton Seafood Shack. Kensi was dressed in a burnt orange sweater dress and a pair of chocolate knee-high boots. She was in a great mood after praying and studying her Bible last night. Her faith was renewed in believing that God was working things out for her.

Dressed in a knee-length blue-jean dress and cowboy boots, the hostess greeted them at the entrance and told them to sit anywhere they liked. Kensi followed Miss Sandra through the half-crowded restaurant as she stopped to greet nearly everyone in their path. Kensi found the neighborly atmosphere to be heartwarming, and something she never experienced while living in New York. She'd be lucky if a stranger returned a smile to her while passing by on the busy sidewalks. This was certainly a change of pace for her.

Miss Sandra finally stopped at a booth next to the window at the back of the restaurant.

"How's this?" Miss Sandra sought Kensi's approval before taking a seat, although she had already placed her purse on the seat.

"It's fine."

Immediately a waitress appeared at their booth to take their drink orders. Kensi ordered a glass of water, while Miss Sandra ordered a sweet tea for the two of them.

"You have to try their sweet tea. It's the best I've ever tasted. It's funny that no other restaurants in town even make it. I swear they look at you like you've grown two heads if you ask for a glass of sweet tea. I'll never forget the looks I got every time I asked for a glass when I first moved here around twenty years ago. You'd think by now, these restaurants would whip up a batch or two. But nope."

"That must be some sweet tea," Kensi commented.

"I'm from Mississippi and we like our tea nice and sweet around there. Around here, you get a glass with two packs of Splenda. I just can't take it," Miss Sandra half-joked. Kensi couldn't help but think of the old TV series *The Golden Girls* whenever Miss Sandra spoke.

When the waitress returned with their drinks and Kensi took a sip, she had to agree with Miss Sandra. That was absolutely the best sweet tea she'd ever tasted—so good that she'd have to remember to get a glass to go and spend a few extra minutes on the treadmill because of the sugar. After taking their orders, the waitress whisked away once more.

"I can tell you love it! Excuse me from babbling on about my tea. Tell me about you sweetheart."

"I'm a career girl trying to navigate my way to the next level, hence the reason I'm here," Kensi said before taking a sip of tea, surprised at the change of pace. At their first meeting, Miss Sandra did most of the talking, but to shift the conversation about her was not what Kensi expected. "That's great, but no husband or fiancé?"

"No." Kensi shook her head as she said it. She didn't want to go down that road in this conversation and she hoped that Miss Sandra would take a hint.

"I don't want to get all in your business, but it'll be nice to have someone to love and support you on your way up to this next level you're trying to get to," Miss Sandra advised.

Kensi nodded through Miss Sandra's speech and was grateful when she changed the subject back to her career and educational background.

"So how does Pepperton fit into the picture?"

Without showing her bitterness toward not getting the promotion she wanted, she shared the story of how she ended up there and what she hoped to gain from the experience. Above all else, she would remain positive and look for the good in the situation; it couldn't be all bad.

"Well Miss Jacobson, I think you'd be a great fit to take over the temporary position at *Pepperton Quad*," Miss Sandra said and smiled.

Kensi's eyes grew wide with amazement. Her first thought was to ask how she knew about her interest, but how could she not? It was a small town and she was one of the executives. *So was this an interview?*

"I figured I'd vet you myself, and this was the perfect opportunity. Well, the second. I've heard about how well you're doing with the trainees and that's no surprise, plus I watched you at the volunteer event with Darren as well. You're already getting along great with the staff and you have the perfect credentials. I don't see any reason why this wouldn't flow seamlessly with your current duties. You have the potential to go as far as you want to go in this industry."

Kensi thanked Miss Sandra as a wide grin covered her face. Her scheduled interview tomorrow would be for her to fill out paperwork and get acquainted with staff she'd be working with. Again, everything seemed to be falling into place for her, and for that she was grateful.

When their lunch arrived, Kensi was glad that Miss Sandra talked her out of ordering a salad; the crab fingers and dirty rice looked delicious. Miss Sandra ordered mahi mahi with a side of rice pilaf. Kensi bowed her head and silently prayed over her food. Before she could take a bite of her own food, Miss Sandra insisted that Kensi try her fish, and again Kensi was glad that she did. Pepperton Seafood Shack had just won over a new customer. They spent the next forty-five minutes chatting about the *Pepperton Quad* and what Kensi should expect over the next few days. After bidding their good-byes, Kensi could think of only one person she wanted to share the news with—Darren.

∞

"I had an interview with *Pepperton Quad* for a temporary position to help with their media presence," Kensi told Samantha.

She'd stood in front of the mirror for the last hour rehearsing how she would tell Samantha about the opportunity. It wasn't going to be a conflict of interest, but she was still nervous as to how Samantha would take the news.

"Kensi, I know I've told you this numerous times, but I feel the need to tell you again. You are amazingly talented. I don't want you to ever feel like you can't spread your wings. Choosing Adam for the assistant editor-in-chief position has nothing to do with your abilities. I hope you understand that."

Kensi shook her head and then said, "I do, thanks." She breathed a sigh of relief. She wasn't sure what she was expecting, but was glad that Samantha seemed to be on board.

"I know that this assignment won't take up all of your time and this will be an excellent opportunity for your career growth. Maybe you'll learn something to help make us better. Anything you need from me, just ask."

"Th-thank you," Kensi stumbled over her words a bit.

"No problem. We value your hard work here, Kensi. I don't want you to ever doubt that," Samantha encouraged, pausing for a moment. The flashing red light on her desk phone alerted her to another call. "Is there anything else?"

"No, I'm fine. Thanks Samantha."

"Again, you're welcome. I appreciate you giving me a courtesy call. Please keep me posted—on the story and the gig at *Pepperton Quad*."

Agreeing, Kensi ended the call and stood watching herself in the mirror. She grinned, thinking about how everything seemed to be working itself out.

Chapter 11

Butterflies danced around in Kensi's stomach as she walked toward the double-door entrance. She nearly fell over when she pulled the door a little bit too forcefully and it didn't open. She had been so preoccupied with trying to calm her nervousness that she forgot that a keycard was needed to access the building, and she'd left hers in her hotel room. She took a step back and pulled her cellphone out of the inside pocket of her purse to phone Miss Sandra.

"Is that you, Kensi?" Miss Sandra's country voice sang from behind her. "Looks like perfect timing." Miss Sandra reached past her, swiped her keycard and held the door open for a fumbling Kensi.

"Whoa!" she exclaimed, juggling her phone to keep from dropping it to the ground. "Thanks, I was just calling you."

"No problem. I can walk you up. You'll just need to sign in with the security guard over to the right since you don't have your badge with you today."

Kensi had completely missed the buzzer to the left of the entrance. She shook her head to get rid of the fuzziness. Today was her first day in her new role and she needed to be on her A game. After giving her driver's license to the security guard to scan for her visitor's pass, she followed Miss Sandra to the elevator bank.

Waiting on the elevator to arrive, Kensi took note of the illuminated advertisement for the *Pepperton Quad* plastered next to the elevators. Her impression that their organization was behind times when it came to media was quickly dwindling. She had to kick herself when she realized the only reason she thought they were limited was that they were located in a small town.

The ding and opening of the elevator reeled her mind back to the present.

"You'll get your own office space for a while now. I'll show you where it is and then we can get you started," Miss Sandra said as they stepped onto the elevator. She pressed the number 7 and turned away from the doors to gaze at the landscape across from their building as they made their way up to the seventh floor.

"Sometimes distance allows us to see things more clearly, doesn't it? When I drive by that pasture, it doesn't look like much, but when I'm up here, I can see all the beauty it has to offer," Miss Sandra commented.

"It is beautiful," Kensi said, turning her head in Miss Sandra's direction to see the green field. Many shades of yellow, blue and pink flowers covered the area; it reminded her of a well painted mural.

The elevator stopped and dinged. Kensi followed Miss Sandra off the elevator and allowed her to lead the way. They walked directly across the hall and entered a set of double glass doors next to an illuminated picture of Pepperton's editor-in-chief plastered on the front page of the local paper.

Kensi's eyes grew wide when she saw Darren being escorted in her direction by a handsome older gentleman. Miss Sandra introduced Kensi to Sterling, the director of marketing. He'd just returned from paternity leave, so she hadn't had a chance to formally meet him before now. They exchanged pleasantries and handshakes with a promise from Sterling to see her later.

"Great to see you again, Kensi," Darren said, shaking her hand as well, probably holding it a second too long, admiring her polished look of a well-tailored blazer and coordinating slacks.

"Same here. I'll be checking in with you later about your project," she informed him and smiled, while Sterling and Miss Sandra watched the exchange.

"I'll be looking forward to it. Have a great day," he said, returning the smile. So many things to tease her about behind that smile, but he left it at that. From the looks of it, he assumed that she was enjoying Pepperton way more than she let on.

"Later." She waved good-bye and nodded to Miss Sandra that she was ready to proceed. She wondered what he could be doing there, but the thought of the holiday festivities quickly approaching and his walking with the marketing director helped answer her question. Even though it was a well-known, annual local event, marketing was still a must.

Miss Sandra and Kensi continued down the corridor until Miss Sandra stopped at a room and opened the door for Kensi. "This is for you. I'll give you a moment to get settled, while I do the same, and then we'll get started." And with that, Miss Sandra left Kensi to unpack her things and settle into the empty office. She only had her purse, tablet, and portfolio. There wasn't much she could do, other than browse the old stack of newspapers piled up in the corner, so she settled in to do so.

"Knock, knock," Miss Sandra sang, simultaneously tapping on the door. "Ready?"

"Sure am!" Kensi answered, tossing the papers to the side to join Miss Sandra at the door, grateful that it only took Miss Sandra about fifteen minutes to return. They walked back to Sterling's office.

"You'll be working with Sterling, so I'll leave you here so that he can get you started. I'll leave instructions for you to fill out your new-hire paperwork online. Don't hesitate to stop by my office if you need anything."

Kensi thanked her and walked into Sterling's office, where Darren occupied one of the empty seats across from his desk.

"I can come back when you're done, if you need me to." The butterflies that she'd managed to get under control were back in full effect.

"Oh no, come right on in. This is perfect. Your first project will be collaborating with Darren over here. And since it seems you two are already working together, it should pan out just fine," Sterling offered.

Kensi took the empty seat next to Darren. His cologne wafted its way to her nostrils. He smelled good, as always. She didn't imagine she'd have to be spending more time with him; she thought that taking this second gig would give her something else to do other than think about him, but instead it seemed that everything that she had on her plate was doing just the opposite.

Chapter 12

Darren stood to the side of the door, holding it open so that Kensi could pass through. Kensi thanked him and smiled, holding his gaze and noticing how the sunlight illuminated his dark brown eyes.

"Apparently a lot has happened since I saw you at the auditorium a few days ago, huh?" Darren asked, his eyes darting around the area, checking their surroundings as he walked with her to the parking lot. The town had ears everywhere, and although Kensi working at *Pepperton Quad* was not a secret, he wanted to have a private conversation with her.

"Yea, things are getting interesting to say the least," Kensi answered.

"Are you moving to Pepperton? Did I miss something?"

"Heavens, no! I'd be bored out of my mind. Working here is just a temporary thing, that's all. With the production still a few weeks away, I needed something else to keep me busy and this opportunity sort of fell into my lap."

"Umm hmm."

"What is that supposed to mean?" Kensi asked, playfully brushing her shoulder up against his, nearly pushing him off the concrete walkway.

"You love it here. You're just afraid to admit it. And even if not, working with me has got to count for something, right?"

Kensi chuckled. She didn't want him to know that working with him was actually the best part of both assignments, but also the most conflicting, so she changed the subject.

"Speaking of working with you, I thought of a theme phrase we could use for the Pepperton Christmas extravaganza. Picture this," she said as she directed his attention toward an imaginary sign with her hands, "Christmas in Pepperton: Connecting the Community through Faith and Fellowship."

"I like that! It will make a good headline in the paper, plus I think it captures the essence of what we're doing here. Thank you."

"Sure, no problem. So you have the day off? Shouldn't you be teaching class or something?"

"Someone hasn't been paying attention. This *is* work. This production means a lot to the folks around here, and a lot of accommodations have been made to make it happen. Hence the reason I'm here and not in the classroom. Besides, this is my conference period."

"Noted."

Kensi stopped at her rental car, opened the door and tossed her things over to the passenger seat.

"Say, umm, are you available around seven tonight? We can meet up for dinner and brainstorm ways to jumpstart the social-media campaign. I'm sure you can handle it, but it would probably be helpful to have someone who's knowledgeable about the project to help you get started, don't you think?" Darren suggested, wanting to kick himself for babbling. What was he doing? Trying to persuade her to go out with him?

"Sounds like a good idea. Work is what I'm here for, right?" she teased.

"I'll give you a call in about an hour so that we can decide on where to eat."

"I met Miss Sandra at Pepperton Seafood Shack earlier this week. Let's go there, if you don't mind."

Darren agreed and tapped the top of the car when she was safely inside, took a few steps back and watched as she pulled out of the parking lot. Pretty soon, he was going to have to come up with another excuse to spend time with her. This event wasn't going to go on forever.

The piddle paddling that she and Darren were doing was driving Kensi crazy. Work was the primary reason for seeing him, but she'd be lying to herself if she said there wasn't anything more. However, she promised herself that she wouldn't jump the gun on whatever they had going. She would wait to see where their connection and the circumstances constantly putting them in each other's path would lead them, though the thought of entertaining a long-distance relationship was enough to make her think twice.

∞

The sweet tea that Miss Sandra insisted she try had been calling her name since the first sip, and was what she planned to order as soon as the waitress came to take their drink orders.

They were nestled in a small booth in the back of the restaurant, closer to the speaker system than Kensi would have liked. Old Reba McEntire tunes seemed to be the only thing in rotation. Darren offered to switch seats with her since it was obvious that she was agitated by the loud music, but she declined. It wasn't so loud that she wouldn't be able to have a conversation with him, but way more volume than she would have liked while sitting down for dinner.

The chandelier that hung just above their table made Darren feel like they were under the spotlight. He constantly dabbed away at beads of perspiration that kept forming on his forehead because of the heat that it was giving off.

"I don't really want to talk about work tonight," Darren said, surprising himself at his candidness.

Kensi's head shot up from the menu, her eyebrows wrinkled in confusion.

"I want to know more about you. We've been talking about work for the last few weeks. I'd really like to get to know you better," Darren continued. He shimmied out of his blazer and laid it in the space next to him. "Only if you're okay with that though," he added when Kensi's face was still clouded with confusion. When she smiled, he relaxed.

"Sounds good to me."

"Tell me about your faith," said Darren.

"Jesus hung, bled and died for my sins and I try to live my life according to His Word," Kensi answered without hesitation. That was definitely not the first question she was expecting. As she thought about it, she realized that no one had ever asked her that before. Adam was the most recent guy she dated, but they never really talked about religion.

"Well Amen to that. That is something we can agree on. What denomination were you raised in?"

"Baptist. But growing up and really experiencing God for myself, denominations haven't mattered much to me. As long as the Bible is being taught, I can work with any church. Back in New York, my church is non-denominational."

"I was raised Baptist as well, and I've never been to a church that isn't. That's not to say that I won't, I just haven't."

"I see. So what are your thoughts about women and their roles in the church?" Kensi asked.

"I believe that God can and will use anyone He chooses to do what He wants done. There were quite a few women in the Bible that He used to carry out His will. Deborah in the book of Judges. Queen Esther and the women in the book of Ruth. And of course, the virgin Mary, Jesus' mother."

"But don't you think they were more of an exception and not the rule?"

"Maybe, but a man couldn't have birthed Jesus, right?"

Kensi chuckled softly.

"So we have to agree that there are certain things that only women can do. I don't think that women should be silent or anything like that. We all have a role to play, we just need to know what it is. So what are your thoughts when it comes to submission in marriage?"

Is everyone going to interview me over dinner? Kensi wondered, because that surely felt like an interview question.

Just then the waitress appeared and took their orders. When she left, Kensi answered his question.

"All right, so you want to know what I think about submission. Great question. I think that as long as a husband is following God, and by that I mean living according to God's Word and doing what he's supposed to do, as his wife, I could easily respect and submit to him. Now if he isn't handling things the way he should, I'm not sure how I would respond in such a situation. But I do agree with the principle. In every organization, someone has to be the leader and I don't think it should be any different in the household. What are your thoughts?"

"Hmm," Darren moaned and nodded. He liked what he heard.

"That's not an answer."

"Sorry, I was just thinking about what you said. I think that men were created to lead. God created Adam first and gave him charge over every living thing before He created Eve. I think that husbands and wives should run their households together, but the ultimate responsibility rests with the husband to do what God calls men to do: Obey Him and love their wives as Christ loves the church."

The waitress returned with their food. At the interruption, Darren reached across the table for Kensi's hand and prayed over their food.

Kensi thought he looked even more handsome, seeing as though he appeared to be a man after God's heart. She was happy that their evening didn't turn out to be about work. She was enjoying their conversation and becoming even more intrigued by him.

As they continued their talk about their beliefs and careers, Darren was in total awe of the woman sitting before him. To meet a godly woman who was beautiful, confident and driven was a treat for him. He'd been so caught up with work and what he'd lost in Jessica that he hadn't even allowed himself to look at anyone in a romantic way before now. Kensi could be the perfect woman for him, except that she was only there temporarily and moving to Pepperton seemed to be the farthest thing from her mind.

Chapter 13

The constant blaring of the bullhorn jolted Kensi out of her sleep. Turning over to look at the alarm clock, she was half-heartedly thankful for the interruption. Two weeks before Christmas, Pepperton's parade kicked off the official festivities for *A Pepperton Christmas,* and she nearly missed it because she set her alarm for PM instead of AM. She needed to take pictures for the *Pepperton Quad*'s social media campaign. If she hurried, she could get photos of the bands, dancers, cheerleaders, Girl Scouts and everyone else before the parade started. She'd probably even get a chance to see Darren with members of the basketball team preparing to ride on a float in the parade.

Dressed in a black cowl-neck sweater, blue jeans, and tall black riding boots with her hair tied back in a low ponytail, she was ready within twenty minutes. She grabbed a blueberry muffin and banana from the complimentary breakfast bar downstairs and headed to the street. The parade line-up began about four blocks away from the hotel.

After gobbling down her breakfast and throwing the banana peel and muffin wrapper in the trash, she pulled out the cell phone and began snapping pictures as she got closer to JROTC, carrying the U.S. and Texas flags. Next in line was Darren's float.

"Can we get a picture for Instagram?" Darren called out to her. About fifteen basketball players were positioned on the float behind him, some of them already posting pictures to social media. He called them together to get in the shot.

"It depends on how interesting this is," Kensi answered, walking around the float as if to determine if it was worthy enough for her to snap a photo of it. It was decorated in the school colors of maroon and white, plastered with signs that boasted of their championship status.

"So, did we pass the test?" John, a senior on the team, called out after she'd circled the float.

Kensi smiled and shrugged, tapping her chin, pretending to think for a moment.

"Oh c'mon! Surely we're the pride and joy of this town. Undefeated for three years in a row and it doesn't hurt that we're the best-looking team around here either," Tommy, the team captain, called to her, tugging on his letterman jacket.

"Is that right?" Kensi looked from Darren to the rest of the team, who were all waiting for her response.

"Well, since you put it that way. Act natural."

Just as Darren and his team were about to protest, Kensi snapped the camera. "Perfect," she said after reviewing the photo. "I'll see you guys later," she called over her shoulder.

When Kensi was out of earshot, Tommy positioned himself on one knee next to Darren and proceeded to give his unsolicited advice in a hushed tone, "Coach, she's beautiful! That's who you've been working with all this time! If I were you, I wouldn't let her get away."

"Dude, you're seventeen! You don't know anything about relationships. Get back there to your team and make sure everyone is good…Captain."

"All right. Don't say I didn't try to help."

Darren chuckled under his breath at the thought of a seventeen year old attempting to give him advice. Although it was good advice, it was none of Tommy's business. As far as Darren was concerned, he had it all under control.

Next stop was the Pepperton High School's marching band, which was warming up playing the scales. She snapped photos of the marching band and the flag twirlers and majorettes, who took a moment to pose for the camera and wish the town a Merry Christmas. Kensi remembered playing the clarinet in ninth grade, being a flag twirler in tenth grade, and performing as a majorette in eleventh and twelfth grade. That photo would be easy to caption, she thought, briefly overcome with nostalgia.

Moving along to another float presented by the Boys and Girls Club of America, Kensi snapped their photos and continued along to the Girl Scouts, school choirs and social and civic clubs. She could hear the band playing "Get Ready" as she trekked alongside the line-up. That song always gave her goose bumps. Although this was her favorite time of the year, she had been a little grumpy in the beginning because she had to spend it in Pepperton, but the town was growing on her as she continued to take part in the festivities.

When the parade started, she walked along the sidelines and took pictures here and there of the Girl Scouts, middle school marching band, cheerleaders, and the beautiful Christmas-decorated floats sponsored by the church, high school clubs, government and civic organizations. It was nothing like the big city Christmas parades that she was used to, but she'd have to give them their props. They did a great job putting it together; she even enjoyed the performances. More and more, she was starting to see that Pepperton wasn't as bad as she made it out to be.

∞

Kensi tugged on her winter hat to cover her ears and held the top of her coat together as she dashed from the car to the auditorium. She hadn't realized that she'd been holding her breath to brace herself against the strong winds. When she reached the door, Darren greeted her.

"Why are you all bundled up like it's below zero? I thought this weather would be easy for Miss New York to handle. Isn't that part of why you're so attached to that place?"

"I love it, but I'm not crazy enough not to take care of myself. Getting sick is not on my agenda this holiday season . . . but if you must know, I am loving this."

"I imagined you'd be turning flips, dancing, or something like that in this kind of weather," Darren teased.

"You're not that funny. I hate to burst your bubble," Kensi said.

"Then why is that smirk on your face?"

Moving into the auditorium, her breath caught in her throat at the transformation that had taken place inside since she'd last been there. If she didn't know any better, she'd think she stepped into winter wonderland. At the entrance, giant candy canes were on both sides of every door. Lights were strung along the center of the walls all the way up to the stage where the nativity scene graced the center. The stage was covered with fake snow and fresh eight-foot Frasier fir trees on either end, decorated with lights, bows and ornaments, all in shades of red and gold.

Some of the student volunteers were putting the final touches on signage while the rest were rehearsing one last time before their performance tomorrow evening.

"This is beautiful," Kensi exclaimed, pulling out the cell phone issued to her by *Pepperton Quad*. She never imagined there would be a point in her career when she'd be getting paid to post on social media.

"The students worked hard putting this together. I'm glad you like it."

"I'm sure the rest of the world will love it too, once I've snapped, posted and hashtagged these photos," Kensi said, walking around the auditorium snapping photos of the scenery, with Darren by her side. She was so impressed that she didn't even take the time to get out of her coat. She went straight to work. Every now and then she stopped to jot down notes on a small notepad that she kept in her coat pocket. The pictures would also go along nicely with the article she was writing for Samantha Elkins.

"Anything I can help you with?" Darren asked. He didn't feel like she needed him much now since she'd hardly said a word since she started taking pictures.

"I think I got it from here. I just wanted to stop by to get a few pictures for social media. I'll see you at the Christmas tree lighting tonight, unless you need something from me."

Darren shrugged. "You've got it all taken care of from the looks of it. I'll walk you back to your car when you're ready."

Kensi prepared her hat and coat once more to brace herself against the wind, while Darren only covered his head with a knit cap before opening the door to escort Kensi to her car.

Despite the cold weather, the brisk walk to the car was too quick for Darren. He wished she was staying longer.

"Want to grab a cup of coffee or hot chocolate after the tree lighting tonight?" Darren asked, licking his lips as he anticipated her answer. His lips were drying out because of the air.

"Sure, that sounds good. I'll be looking forward to it."

"Later."

Darren tapped on the hood and took a few steps back so that she could pull out of the parking space. He made a dash for the building when she turned the corner, satisfied that he'd secured another opportunity to spend time with Kensi outside of work.

Chapter 14

Pepperton's annual tree lighting ceremony had come to be a popular part of the small town's festivities as the citizens continued the countdown to Christmas Day, now only eight days away. Kensi couldn't believe how far down the road she had to park her car. As far as she had to walk to the center of Pepperton Central Park from her car, she could have very well walked from her hotel. Seeing the crowd reminded her of Madison Square Park Conservancy's annual tree lighting ceremony. Although she despised large crowds, she toughed it out to be front and center for that spectacular event. And though she loved cold weather, that was the only time she voluntarily stood outside in it. In addition to being bundled up with a wool hat, coat, gloves, and scarf, the body heat of all those people usually helped to deal with the freezing temperature.

She walked slowly toward the large huddle amazed at the shimmering red and gold decorations on the tree. To the far left, a band dressed like elves was doing mic checks and tuning their instruments. To the far right, there was a bounce house and crafts for the children. A few neighborhood restaurants were set up on site serving hot chocolate, cookies and soups.

And here I thought that I would miss the Madison Square Park event. It's almost as if it's come to me, Kensi thought.

The vibration of the cell phone in her coat pocket reminded her that she should be taking photos of the event. She'd almost forgotten that she wasn't simply a spectator, but this was work for her. She silenced the vibration, opened the camera app, and started capturing moments.

She couldn't help but notice that everyone seemed content and at peace. This was home for them. Chatter from adults and squeals from children nearly drowned out the sounds of the holiday music playing. She watched and snapped pictures as more townspeople joined the huddle, hugging everyone in their immediate circle as if they hadn't seen them in years, while the small children who accompanied them darted off to the craft zone. The maroon colored oversized tent housed face painting and tables covered with art supplies to make Christmas themed crafts. The teenagers who weren't preoccupied on their cellphones or chatting with one another supervised the moonwalks and art projects.

"Nice isn't it?" Miss Sandra seemed to appear out of nowhere and threw an arm around Kensi's shoulder, squeezing tightly. Her smile was as bright as the Christmas lights strewn around the park. "You're going to enjoy this, so try to get work out of the way so that you can be a part of the celebration!" Miss Sandra's voice made her ears throb, as she screamed over the crowd and music into Kensi's ear.

Kensi nodded after Miss Sandra gave another gentle squeeze and disappeared into the crowd just as quickly as she appeared a moment ago. Joy filled the atmosphere as she witnessed genuine hugs and smiles and children enjoying the crafts and games. They were definitely in the holiday spirit.

"You look like you're in your element!" Darren called to her from behind.

Kensi's head snapped around at the sound of his voice.

"You could say that. Why didn't you tell me how nice this was going to be? I was thinking that you all would be gathered around the tree singing Christmas carols or something. Light the tree, sing 'kum ba yah' and go home."

"You think so little of us around here, don't you?"

They both chuckled.

"Nah, it's just that it's a small town, so I expected something small, I guess. But this," she exclaimed and gestured, "is like baby New York!"

"I'm not sure if that's a compliment or not. Just because this isn't a big city doesn't mean we cannot do nice things. There's a lot of love around here. You just need to take some time to see that."

"Noted," Kensi said, lifting her camera to take more pictures while Darren stood by her side.

"You know I can help you with the social media caption on those . . . or for the paper or whatever."

Kensi squinted and thought for a moment. Clearly, he didn't understand how easy a task this was, or perhaps he thought she was social-media challenged. She didn't get the job because she needed help with captions. She was a journalist for goodness sake. Surely she could come up with a catchy caption.

"Well . . . only if there's something special that you'd like to say about all of this. It has to be something that I couldn't come up with on my own."

"Okay, so—"

"And you'd better do it fast, because these pics are going up in just a moment," Kensi interrupted him.

When Kensi finished her pre-ceremony pictures, she and Darren walked over to a nearby park bench so that she could sit for a moment and start blasting the pictures on social media. Even though it was an easy task, she was glad that she had his company. He actually had a couple of catchy things to say about the event, to Kensi's surprise.

In the distance, Kensi and Darren could hear Mayor Thomas Wentworth speaking. "Each year, I look forward to the moment when I can stand before you and witness your smiling faces as we celebrate the holiday season. As always, I hope that this season is filled with love and joy and that you approach it with a spirit of expectancy . . ." he went on.

Kensi and Darren remain seated listening to the mayor and watching as the shimmering lights began to glow on the Christmas tree and a parade of fireworks lit the evening sky, drawing the children away from their designated area. On cue, the band started playing their version of "We Wish You a Merry Christmas." The crowd joined in with the band singing the famous tune.

Kensi was glad to be a part of Pepperton's Christmas. But she still couldn't understand why Samantha wanted to cover it in *The Big Apple Arts Chronicle*. There had to be something that she was missing.

∞

It seemed as if most of the town had the same idea to head to the coffee shop after the tree lighting ceremony. There was only one table left in the place and it was closer to the door than they would have liked. Kensi held the table while Darren ordered their drinks. He returned to the table with a goofy smile plastered across his face. He draped his jacket over her shoulders and took the seat across from her.

"I'm sorry. This is not what I pictured when I asked you to have coffee with me. I was thinking nice and cozy, not dodging wind chills. I won't keep you here too long." Spending a few moments with her here and there wasn't working for him anymore. It was time he did something about that before it was too late.

"Believe it or not, I'm okay." She smiled to reassure him.

Kensi wrapped her hands around the mug of caramel latte sitting in front of her and then rubbed her hands along her arms each time someone walked into the coffee shop. The gush of wind gave her chills and temporarily drowned out the sound of the holiday music playing over the speakers.

"You're not the New Yorker I thought you were," Darren teased.

"What kind of New Yorker did you think I was?"

Darren peered over his cup of hot chocolate at Kensi, careful to keep his eyes locked on hers while he took a sip. He could go on and continue beating around the bush about how he felt, but he knew all too well that the next minute wasn't promised. He thought he had forever with Jessica and that proved not to be true.

"How about we not worry about what I thought and let me get a chance to see for myself? I want to date you, Kensi, seriously and exclusively, once your assignment is over."

Kensi's eyes grew wide with surprise. She took several sips of her latte to compose her thoughts and contemplate her response. She was aware that he was fond of her, and that feeling was mutual. However, she wasn't expecting him to be so direct. In a matter of seconds, her mind went into complete overdrive as she pondered her decision. If she said *no*, that would go against all the whining that she'd done to God a few weeks ago about *her turn for happiness.* But saying *yes* could mean that she would likely have to move to Pepperton if things went well. She'd need a new job. She'd have to give up New York and months of the cold weather that she loved so much plus she'd be even farther away from her family.

She closed her eyes for a moment to calm down and reel her mind back into the present. Although those things were important, that could easily be worked out later. She liked him, so she owed it to herself to see if their relationship could grow wings.

"I'd like that too," she finally answered.

"Good. You had me worried here for a second," Darren said with a nervous chuckle. "I'm looking forward to spending more time getting to know the woman behind the camera and the pencil."

"Of course you are!" Kensi joked, breaking up the seriousness of the moment.

Darren reached across the table and squeezed her hand. Tomorrow was the theatrical production and he had never looked forward to it more than he was now. Closing the curtains after the Christmas program tomorrow set the stage for them to move forward to see what life had in store for the two of them—together.

Chapter 15

"Joy to the World" played softly on the speakers while the stage crew volunteers carefully placed life-sized cutouts of snowflakes, angels, horns, and trees around the auditorium. It was one hour until showtime and Kensi had started to look forward to the program, since the tree lighting and parade had impressed her so.

Darren sat on the steps leading up to the stage, listening to Jamie, Sasha, and David, who were portraying the three wise men, run their lines for the play. Though they knew their lines, they were a little afraid, since it would be the first time any of them had been on stage.

"Great job guys," Darren encouraged them, "but do one little favor for me. Stretch your arms wide and shake your hands."

Jamie, Sasha, and David looked confused, but followed his instructions.

"Now jog in place before I release you to go eat some of Mrs. Caldwell's homemade chocolate chip cookies."

The timid voices that Darren heard minutes ago were replaced with high pitched yeses and cheering upon hearing about Mrs. Caldwell's cookies.

"Just kidding guys. There aren't any cookies in the back that I know about, but that's the enthusiasm we need to see and feel onstage. Got it?"

"Got it," they said in unison, clearly disappointed.

"I should have known that was too good to be true. I don't smell any cookies," Sasha pointed out.

"I'm so proud of you guys. I know you'll do well. Now go to the back and let Mrs. Caldwell adjust your costumes. Who knows? There may be cookies later."

Kensi applauded his attentiveness to the students as she sat in the front row middle section and watched the interaction. Darren had stopped by to make sure she was comfortable and to offer his help if needed, but spent most of his time making sure everything was ready. Kensi looked up every now and again to take notice of the last-minute preparations going on around her. Otherwise she jotted down notes from the tree lighting ceremony, flipping through the pictures she'd taken to jog her memory every now and then.

She had a couple of weeks left in town, since her temporary assignment with the *Pepperton Quad* extended through the end of the year, then she planned to take a couple of vacation days before going back to New York in January, unless Samantha gave her an assignment that whisked her off to some other unknown place. But she promised herself she wouldn't worry much about any of that right now. She would spend time getting to know Darren over the Christmas and New Year holidays.

"Isn't this lovely?" Miss Sandra interrupted Kensi's musings. She didn't realize that she'd stopped writing and had started tapping the notepad with her pencil.

"Yes, it is! I can't wait to see the production!"

"Samantha getting you away from my nephew wasn't so bad after all, was it? Pepperton is treating you really good. Darren can't stop looking over here at you, and you're doing an amazing job over at *Pepperton Quad.* Seems like this was just the change you needed, right?" Miss Sandra rambled in her country voice.

Kensi blinked several times as if that would help everything make sense. Nephew? Samantha?

"Who is your nephew?" Kensi asked, focusing on what Miss Sandra had just revealed.

"Adam! You didn't know that?"

"No," Kensi answered, shaking her head slowly. *That is why Miss Sandra acts and looks familiar. This was a setup the entire time.* Getting passed up for the promotion. Getting sent to Pepperton, Texas. The temporary assignment for *Pepperton Quad.* Samantha Elkins' hands were all over this.

"Were you part of Samantha's plan?" Kensi asked. She forced back the tears and swallowed the lump that was forming in her throat. She had known that something wasn't right.

Why would she need to come all the way to Pepperton? Seems like she was given some fake assignment just so that Samantha could get rid of her—and that was an insult to her intelligence. And for what? To get her off Adam's radar?

"Oh no, honey! I don't meddle in people's lives to that magnitude. That was all her. But it worked out, right?" Miss Sandra searched for a way to back out of the conversation. She hadn't realized that Kensi didn't know she was related to Samantha and Adam.

"No worries." Kensi took a deep breath before continuing. "It has worked out in my favor and I'm quite thankful for that." But she wasn't thankful for Samantha's dishonesty. And even though things had been coming together like pieces to a puzzle, what gave Samantha the right to interfere with her life this way? How was she going to handle that when she returned to the office? *If* she returned. *Did Adam know?* And if he did, would he tell her?

Miss Sandra gave Kensi a reassuring tap on the shoulder and slipped away. She didn't know all the details surrounding Samantha sending Kensi to town, and she wasn't sure if she wanted to know. She wouldn't worry about it for now. If nothing else, she believed wholeheartedly that God had a way of using people to get things done, whether we agreed with their methods or not.

Darren was onstage doing final mic checks when he noticed the sullen look on Kensi's face. He saw her talking with Miss Sandra and wondered if their conversation was the reason for Kensi's grin disappearing. He made a beeline to her seat as soon as he finished.

"Are you all right?" he asked.

"Yeah, I'm good. Anxious to see the performances this evening. Are y'all ready?" Kensi asked, dismissing Darren's concern. She was still trying to make sense of her conversation with Miss Sandra and discussing it at that moment wasn't going to resolve the uneasiness she felt.

"Sit tight and you'll see." Darren brushed her hand with a kiss and left her side to go backstage. Since they were planning to get to know each other better, he'd find out what happened sooner or later.

Moments later, the only lights shining were the stage lights and the string lights that were hung around the building. Darren appeared onstage and thanked everyone for their support. Kensi peered over her shoulder and saw the auditorium filled with guests. Though she had heard the chatter, she had no idea the auditorium had filled so quickly. She had been so caught up with what Miss Sandra had just revealed that she completely missed everything happening around her. No matter the rationale regarding her being in Pepperton, she was going to enjoy it and do what she was sent there to do.

The thunder of applause pulled her out of her thoughts once more, and she settled into her seat with her *Pepperton Quad* issued phone, ready to enjoy the performances and snap pictures for social media; *Pepperton Quad*'s photographer's photos would be used for the digital paper they were working to produce.

A sixth grader with a powerful voice opened the program singing "Mary Did You Know." Kensi had never heard it sung so beautifully. When the little girl had finished, Kensi's eyes were filled with tears, along with most of the members of the audience.

The moment she exited the stage, the dance troupe entered, dressed in all black with red accessories, with children ranging from ages five to twelve. Their praise dance was right on cue with every lyric from "Now Behold the Lamb." Kensi was amazed at how well choreographed the dance was and how well the children executed it. She continuously had to remind herself to take pictures.

The high school chorus entered the stage following the exit of the dance troupe. They performed several Christmas songs: "Do You Hear What I Hear?" "Silent Night," "Hark the Herald Angels Sing," and "Twelve Days of Christmas." During "Twelve Days of Christmas," children ranging from five to twelve marched from backstage into the audience and presented their parents with small handmade gifts. Kensi thought it was the cutest thing she ever saw. She had to get out of her seat to capture the moment. Some parents were genuinely surprised at the gesture, though it was something they'd done in years past.

Kensi was impressed at how seamlessly the program ran. Performance after performance, whether singing, dancing, or reciting poetry, the students entered and exited the stage with ease as if they'd been doing it all year long.

The most beautiful performance was the story of Jesus' birth. Gone was the nativity scene that graced the stage during the other performances, and in its place was the nativity set that was built by the students specifically for the play. The student actors were so convincing as the inn keeper, Mary, Joseph, the angel and the three wise men. Ever so softly, the rest of the students sang "Silent Night" in the background while those in the nativity scene performed. If there was anyone who hadn't shed a tear earlier that night, they did after that performance. It was apparent that the students knew the story or took the time to study it, because they performed it well.

As much as she loved New York, Kensi had never witnessed such an awesome performance by young people in the big city.

The event ended with all student performers on stage singing "We Wish You a Merry Christmas." One by one, the students exited both sides of the stage while continuing to sing. The lights brightened in the auditorium as each student picked up a small basket from those set on both ends of the stage and handed out small wrapped boxes to everyone present. Each box contained a piece of chocolate, an encouraging note, and a handmade ornament. Once again Kensi got caught up in the excitement and had to remind herself to take pictures.

Darren returned from backstage and thanked everyone for their support and allowing their children to participate.

"It is such an honor to work with the youth. You all may not believe it, but they put most of this together. Most of the time, I was merely the adult in the room, so you should be proud of the young people in your life. You have such amazing children." Darren paused while the crowd burst into a round of applause. He eyed Kensi, who had just put the camera down to clap as well.

"Most of you know we have a special visitor in town who came from the big city to check us out this year. I hope we exceeded her expectations. Kensi Jacobson, would you like to say a few words?"

Kensi shook her head and mouthed *no,* but Darren insisted she come onstage anyway. Reluctantly, she moved from her seat to meet Darren onstage. He gave her his hand as she walked up the steps and handed the mic to her.

"You all are *so* amazing; and I don't think I've ever seen a show this well organized and performed. You aren't even my babies and I'm so proud of each of you," Kensi praised them. After thanking them for their hospitality while she had been in Pepperton, she handed the mic back to Darren and returned to her seat.

"She's amazing as well and we're happy to have her here too, isn't that right P-town?" Darren asked the crowd, who cheered in response. He bid the crowd good night and joined Kensi at her seat.

"What did your special note say?" Darren asked.

Kensi opened the box wrapped in shiny red giftwrap and pulled out the contents: a round, shiny, maroon ornament with the words "Merry Christmas" written in white gel ink, a Hershey's kiss, and a note with the scripture, Joshua 1:9, "Have I not commanded you? Be strong and courageous. Do not be afraid; do not be discouraged, for the Lord your God will be with you wherever you go." She read the scripture aloud to Darren as she allowed the words to sink down in her spirit. Timely. That was exactly what she needed in that moment after the talk she'd had with Miss Sandra. No matter where she is, God was always with her and His plans always prevailed.

"Amen," Kensi said after reading the scripture. A sentiment in which Darren echoed.

"His Word is always on time. Am I right?"

"You have no idea."

Satisfied with seeing the light return to her eyes, he nodded toward the phone. "May I see if you've done us any justice on social media?"

"Sure," Kensi answered, opening up the Instagram app so that he could see the pictures she posted.

"And so it begins, right?" he asked and smiled, handing the phone back to her. His smile was as big as the auditorium. That was the end of the *Pepperton Christmas* production, and now was the time for them to put that same energy into getting to know each other better.

"It does." Kensi's smile matched his as she tucked the phone and notes away, linked her arm into his and strolled with him out of the auditorium. She was reminded of the Scripture in Ecclesiastes that says, "There is a time for everything, and a season for every activity under the heavens." She hoped that this was the season for her to experience the happiness that she had been dreaming of.

Chapter 16

To get away from the town's eyes, Kensi and Darren went to Houston for their first official date. After early morning church service, they set off to spend the day having fun without everyone in Pepperton watching their every move. They wanted to enjoy each other's company without the questioning looks or those who felt comfortable enough to simply ask if they were dating.

Upon Raegan's suggestion, their first stop was at the Breakfast Klub. When they arrived, patrons were standing in a line wrapped around the small yellow building.

"Are you sure we're in the right place?" Darren asked, circling the building trying to find a parking space.

"Yea," Kensi answered, checking the GPS on her phone. "Raegan said there may be a line, but it moves fast. Apparently, that is all part of the experience."

"Well, we have nothing but time today, so let's check it out," Darren said as he pulled into a parking space in a muddy parking lot across the street. "Before you get out, let me come around to check that area near your door. It's quite a bit of mud around here."

Darren dodged a couple of muddy sections in the grass and went around to help Kensi out of the car. Luckily there was only a small puddle of mud near her door and he helped her over it by allowing her to use his arm to steady herself.

The duo walked side by side to the restaurant to get a place in line. Before making it to the end, a familiar voice called out to her. She had been so focused on getting in line that she didn't hear her name until Darren mentioned it. They turned around to see Raegan and Caleb waving to them. She should have expected to see them after mentioning that they would be coming to Houston.

"We saved you guys a spot in line," Raegan said after giving Kensi a tight squeeze. She then whispered to Kensi, "Now you know that I wouldn't have missed the opportunity to see who my friend was taking road trips with, right? I love you," she said and squeezed once more before pulling away.

"Introduce us, Kensi," Caleb interjected.

Kensi shook her head, smiled and proceeded with introductions. Caleb shook hands with Darren and Raegan greeted him with a friendly one-armed hug. Kensi stopped and spoke to the couple standing behind them, because she didn't want people getting offended because they skipped line. The couple was warm and friendly, holding a conversation with the group until they made it to the front of the line to place their orders.

Scanning the menu, Darren asked, "What's good?"

"Everything. You can't go wrong with anything on the menu. Cami got me hooked on this place while she was pregnant. I can't tell you how many times I had to bring her out for the wings and waffles or place a to-go order. They should know us by name as much time and money as we spent here," Caleb answered.

Darren ordered the wings and waffles, while Kensi ordered the shrimp and grits. Raegan and Caleb both ordered the wings and waffles, along with the famous cappuccino. They found an empty table to seat four, sat down and chatted while waiting for their breakfast.

"Darren, I'm sorry we're imposing on your time with Kensi, but when she mentioned that you guys were coming, I suddenly had a taste for wings and waffles. It is *so* good!" Raegan apologized and praised the food.

"They're best friends, Darren. She's not sorry. She's coming to check you out, but the food is good," Caleb countered, and everyone chuckled.

"It's cool. It's probably a good idea that we all get to know each other. Maybe you can convince her to move to Texas."

"Y'all know I'm a city girl, specifically a New York City girl. No Pepperton, Texas, for me," Kensi added. Raegan sat across from her and they had a conversation without saying a word. They both knew that given the right conditions, she'd leave New York.

"We'll see about that," Darren added and took a sip of cappuccino.

Raegan took the reins of the conversation and questioned Darren about his background, where he grew up, why he moved to Pepperton, his future plans and where he saw Kensi fitting into those plans. As much as she enjoyed the food, she didn't stop her interrogation when it arrived.

Darren answered her questions as if he'd been preparing for them his whole life. His responses were perfect, almost too perfect in Raegan's opinion. Though he didn't appear to be the type who would treat Kensi badly, Raegan didn't want this to turn out to be another Rico type situation. He was far from that type, but it made Raegan wonder if he was hiding something too.

"Well that was intense!" Kensi finally added when Raegan finished her line of questioning. Neither Caleb nor Kensi stopped Raegan, only piggybacked on a question here or there.

"Nah it's all good. She's just looking out for you. Any good friend would have done the same thing. Besides, I'd probably be concerned if she didn't grill me like a piece of meat," Darren said and chuckled. The others burst into laughter at his comment and commenced friendly chatter until Raegan and Caleb had to leave and get back to their children.

Caleb and Darren left tips for the waitress before rising from the table and meeting the ladies out front. Kensi and Raegan had walked out just minutes before them, using the excuse of needing to use the restroom to talk privately.

Kensi and Raegan were standing in front of the building to the right of the long line that seemed to have no end. Raegan gave her smile of approval to Kensi after offering a few encouraging words.

"I like him for you, Kens. He seems really nice. I wasn't trying to embarrass you, but you know I've learned my lesson from not asking enough questions."

"Amen. I think our entire circle learned from you," Kensi agreed.

"If I can help you avoid a Rico situation, you best believe I'm going to be inspector gadget."

"And amen again," Kensi agreed and chuckled.

"Bring Darren by again sometime, Kens, if you all have the time," Caleb said when they caught up to the women standing outside. "It was good to meet you bro." Caleb shook Darren's hand once more after the couple hugged Kensi and bid their goodbyes.

When Caleb and Raegan reached their car, Raegan asked, "So what do you really think about him?"

"I think that given enough time, he could be a good match for our little Kensi."

"Stop talking about her as if she's a little girl," Raegan said and giggled after swatting his shoulder. "Maybe she's found her perfect match, just like we did."

Caleb agreed by leaning across the center console and pressing his lips against hers. If Kensi had finally found what they had, she should count herself blessed.

"I guess we'll see. Let's get home to our babies."

Chapter 17

Darren immediately switched on the heat when he and Kensi were back inside the car. He didn't remember it being as cold when they were waiting in line outside of the restaurant.

"That intense huh?" Kensi teased.

Darren chuckled and responded, "It's freezing out there. Are you immune to it today?" He turned on the seat warmer and noticed a low chuckle from Kensi. "I know you aren't talking about your friend and her husband. They were cool people. I like them. Beautiful couple."

"Yeah, you did good. We all appreciated your honesty." Kensi was surprised that he went into so much detail about the death of his late wife. She hadn't asked many questions about that because she wasn't sure how much he was still holding on to her. But based on how he handled himself today and made known how he planned to spend his time courting her, it seemed that he had properly packaged his past.

Darren smiled and nodded at Kensi's compliments. He input the GPS coordinates for their next destination and slowly pulled out of the parking space, careful not to get stuck in the mud.

"You do realize that we're about to go ice skating, right? This little drop in temperature is nothing. Besides, we have our coats. We're prepared for this. . . . At least I thought we were. Is this your way of telling me that you want to back out? Are you afraid to fall on the ice in front of me?" Kensi cooed.

"Fall? Me? No! I'm thinking about you. I don't want you to get sick or anything like that. I'll be blaming myself for ages if that happens."

"Umm hmm. . . Well you have nothing to worry about. I'm in." Kensi's breath was taken away at the sight of Discovery Green's boat basin transformed into an ice park. From the parking space on the curb, Kensi could see the area around the outside rink lit up with red and green holiday lights. The area wasn't crowded yet. Families were just starting to settle in, so the view from their parking space excited Kensi even more.

"This should be fun, especially since I've never ice skated in my entire life."

"Wait, what? This was your idea. I've never ice skated either. I figured you did this sort of thing in New York. So this means we'll be struggling out there together?" Darren concluded and chuckled.

"Looks that way. See, told you this would be fun."

"There's no one else I'd rather be struggling out there on that ice with and potentially breaking bones."

When the couple made the trek from the car to the ice park, Darren had to agree with Kensi that the view was absolutely gorgeous. Passing people who were seated at the tables surrounding the rink shoving their feet into ice skates, Kensi and Darren strolled up to the booth to purchase tickets and collect their rental skates.

"Look at those kids out there," Darren commented and nodded toward the rink. "They're gonna be skating circles around us."

"Sounds like someone is afraid to fall," Kensi sang.

"Pssh. I'm a quick learner, I'll have it down pat in no time."

Darren held onto Kensi's elbow and guided her to an open seat. He strapped on his skates and then helped Kensi, who appeared to be struggling a little. He lifted her right foot, gently placed it across his lap, adjusted the skate until she acknowledged it was comfortable and laced it up for her.

The couple timidly rose to their feet and inched their way toward the ice rink, holding on to the rail that surrounded the rink. Darren stepped onto the ice first, and then held out his hand for Kensi to join him. He immediately slipped on the ice and yelled, "Ouch!"

"This is definitely nothing like roller-skating and much harder than it looks. We can't hold hands. Every man for himself."

Kensi burst into laughter at his sentiments. She felt a little guilty since she had gripped his hand much harder than he anticipated when she stepped on the ice, causing the fall.

"I'm sorry. That was my fault," Kensi said, holding on to the rail. "Let's give this a try." She slowly moved away from Darren, who was recovering from his fall and taking hold of the rails so that it wouldn't happen again.

Darren stayed behind Kensi, pausing every time another skater passed by him. He was not risking falling again. He was embarrassed enough as it was. Kensi didn't seem concerned by it but he was bothered a little. He wanted to make a good impression today, not fall on his butt, literally. He was enjoying himself, but that was definitely not what he had in mind.

"C'mon slow poke! Even Santa is rolling around this rink better than us. We can't let jolly ole Saint Nick outdo us!" Kensi called to Darren behind her.

"I can't compete with Santa today, or else I'll be asking for a new hip for Christmas."

"That's not the *quick learner* spirit I hear. One more lap and we can take a break. I need to get out of this jacket." The sun seemed to have been hovering over the area. They had only been around the rink once, but both were starting to realize that they should probably choose something else to do. They couldn't believe that small children, who couldn't have been more than five or six years old, were doing better than they were. They found laughter in the activity and enjoyed seeing the children having fun, but it was time for them to call it quits.

"Yeah, it's getting hot. What's up with this Houston weather? I was cold not long ago." It was not unusual to experience two different seasons in Houston on any given day, especially during this time of the year.

The duo finally made their way around to the exit and hurriedly got out of the ice skates. Since the weather wasn't as cool as before with the sunlight warming the area, Darren suggested that they picnic in the park, something nice and safe where they could get to know each other just a little bit better.

Chapter 18

"Forgive me for fiddling with my phone, but my cousin keeps texting me," Kensi apologized. Kensi and her cousin Shana practically grew up as sisters. Lately, their jobs had been keeping both of them busy, so they hadn't had a chance to talk. Shana was on her way out of the country on a mission trip to South Africa, along with her fiancé, Eric, and she was trying her best to get Kensi to come home for Christmas. Kensi hadn't celebrated Christmas with her family in two years, once because she was snowed in and another because of work; she used Skype to be there without being there. Even so, she was only half disappointed since she despised having to answer the *why aren't you married or engaged* questions from her entire family; technology had proven to be her friend in helping her avoid the conversation whenever it turned to her relationship status.

"What's up with her?" Darren asked, growing concerned.

Kensi dismissed his question with the wave of her hand and changed the subject to their picnic. "This looks like a nice area. Want to camp out here for a while?" Kensi asked.

They were about a half mile away from the rink. Darren had gone to his car to get a few blankets and now they were trying to find the perfect area to settle.

"Yeah. There are a few food trucks over there. Anything in particular you want to try?"

"I'm being adventurous today. I'll have whatever you're having," Kensi answered.

Darren unfolded the blankets and neatly placed them on the ground. He suggested that Kensi call her cousin while he was away so that they could enjoy the rest of the afternoon as planned without her fidgeting with her phone. He helped her down onto the blanket and went in search of lunch, although it hadn't been that long ago since they ate at the Breakfast Klub. He decided he'd go for something light as he perused the area.

"So, what's up, Shana?" Kensi asked hurriedly when she got her cousin on the line.

"No longer avoiding me, are you?"

"Cut that out. What's going on? I only have a few minutes. I'm on a date."

"Oooh! Is it serious?"

"Stay focused, Shana. What's so urgent? We can talk about all of the date stuff later."

"You read my message! I'm serious. I need you to come home this Christmas!" Shana blurted out. "Before you tune me out, just listen. Please, favorite cousin in the whole wide world!"

Kensi rolled her eyes. She could only imagine the pouty face that Shana was making on the other end of the call. Instead of giving a response, she blew an audibly loud breath and waited for Shana to explain.

"Eric and I have decided to get married over the Christmas holidays before we leave for our mission trip. Since we don't know how God will lead us while we're there, we want our families to share in this special moment in our lives before we go. Who knows? We may never come back! Besides, I miss my favorite cousin. You know that, right?"

"I wouldn't miss it for anything in the world," Kensi responded, trying to muster up enthusiasm. It wasn't as if she wasn't excited for Shana, but she knew she wouldn't be able to avoid all the relationship questions with this wedding business going on. Who's next was always the follow-up conversation after a wedding ceremony.

Shana squealed and promised to call Kensi later to get the details on this new guy she was dating. Kensi ended the call and said to herself, "Get it together. This is not about you."

Kensi wrapped her arms around her knees and allowed her mind to wonder what the holidays were going to be like with her cousin marrying and getting ready to leave the country. Was her family going to expect her to get married next? Who was she kidding? They'd been waiting on that for years now. Her mom constantly spoke of her future grandbabies and hounded Kensi about when she was planning to stop chasing her career and settle down. She should have been looking forward to the festivities with excitement, but instead she felt nothing but anxiety.

"I stopped at a couple of different vendors," Darren said, approaching with bags of fresh breads, cheeses and fresh vegetables.

"What is all this?" Kensi asked, reaching out to help Darren place the items on the purple and gold picnic blanket.

Since they'd recently had breakfast, he only bought foods to snack on. The farmer's market was taking place downtown today, so he patronized a few of the vendors. He settled down on the blanket, opened the bag filled with fresh cheeses, and shared it with Kensi.

"Why the long face? I wasn't gone that long, was I?"

Kensi smiled and said, "Nah, I didn't think so." She didn't realize that her face was reflecting the uneasiness she felt about going home.

"Is your cousin all right?" Darren asked. Kensi thought for a moment and figured she may as well get it off her chest. She shared the reason for the call with Darren and his face lit up. Quite the opposite of how she was feeling, but he didn't understand.

"I do miss my family. I actually hadn't thought much about what I would be doing for Christmas this year anyway. I guess work has kept my mind occupied," she said and silently added, *Along with you.*

"You planned to spend it with me. Admit it," Darren half-joked and plucked a piece of bread in her direction.

"Don't flatter yourself."

"Honesty is the best policy, Miss Jacobson. I'm flexible though. I can come with you if you're going to miss me that much!" Darren teased. "Wait a minute, that's why you had that little pout on your face. You were gonna miss me?" His smile was as wide as the state of Texas.

"Seriously?"

"What?"

"You *want* to go to Virginia with me?" Kensi asked, sounding skeptical.

"At your service."

"Well, I guess it's settled."

Kensi's stomach twisted in knots as her mind raced back and forth at the thought of Darren coming along with her for the holidays. Did she really just agree to that? What was her family going to think? What was he going to think about their relationship and where it was headed? That was a long enough ride to get to know each other more and gain clarity about what they wanted from each other. If nothing else, she would learn whether or not she could stand to be with him for long periods of time. This extra time together could be a good thing. There was no telling where things would be headed when she moved back to New York.

Chapter 19

Two days before Christmas, Kensi checked out of her hotel in Pepperton while Darren waited for her in the lobby. If the townspeople weren't chatting about them before, they were surely chatting now, Darren mused, but he didn't care. He was determined to live his life however he saw fit. Although the townspeople were close and he had spent the holidays participating in local events in the past, he still felt alone without Jessica. He was looking forward to moving out of the shadows of his pain and enjoying this holiday season with someone he was growing to care about.

"Ready to get this show on the road?" Darren asked Kensi as she strolled toward him.

"As ready as I'll ever be. Are you sure about this?"

"Is this your way of trying to leave me in the dust?"

"Ha-ha. Very funny. I'm just trying to make sure you're okay with traveling across the country with a woman you hardly even know."

"I've been working with you for several weeks now. I don't think you'd take advantage of me."

"How do you know I won't leave you at a diner in the middle of nowhere?"

"So is that your plan for me? To love me and leave me?" Darren continued to joke.

Shaking her head and rolling her eyes at his silliness, she said, "Whatever," and gestured for him to load her bags in the rental car.

Darren set her bags on the ground near the trunk and rushed over to open the passenger door for her. He clasped her hands in his as his mood turned from playful to serious.

"Kensi Jacobson. I like you a lot and I care about you. I'm coming along with you to provide support and in hopes that this road trip will give us more time to get to know each other. If you think this is too much too soon, just say the word and I'll grab my things out of the trunk, hand you the keys, hug you good-bye, and see you after Christmas. Just tell me what you want me to do," His eyes were locked on hers, waiting to see if she would change her mind or if she would continue with the road trip as planned. He hoped she wasn't going to leave him behind, because he looked forward to spending the next few days getting to know her better. After all, that was his promise to her: when work was done, he wanted to spend time getting know her on a more personal level. This seemed to be the perfect opportunity to follow through.

Kensi briefly considered calling the whole thing off when he put the option back on the table. She'd known guys who wanted to spend tons of time with her in the beginning to make it seem as if she'd known them for a long time in hopes of her sleeping with them. But Darren seemed sincere; he didn't strike her as that type of guy. She was fond of him and she was sure he wouldn't leave her on the side of the road somewhere. Raegan and Caleb pretty much got every piece of identifying information from him, except his social security number, when she told them they were taking this trip together. If he did something crazy, they would find him.

"I'm good. I just wanted you to be sure that you're okay with this. So if you're cool, I'm cool. Besides, I'm looking forward to getting to know a little more about Darren Shaw, so let's get this party started!" Kensi suggested.

Darren kissed her cheek before he helped her inside, placed the bags in the trunk, walked around to the driver's seat, and hopped in the car. When Darren secured himself inside, he extended his hand so that he and Kensi could pray and ask God to protect them along the way. A wave of assurance washed over Kensi when she intertwined her hand with his. She felt safe with him. When Darren finished the prayer and Kensi echoed "Amen," her heart fluttered. They were really doing this.

They spent the first hour of the ride talking about their favorite past Christmas holidays. They both shared memories of Christmas growing up without siblings, however. Kensi always celebrated with a large family. Aside from growing up celebrating Christmas as a child, the first Christmas he celebrated with Jessica could have easily been the best Christmas ever, but he strayed away from that thought. He hoped to get through this season without grieving her death, and hopefully spending time with Kensi and her family would help him do that. He then changed the subject to play twenty questions to keep from thinking of Jessica and their time together. He spent the next couple of hours listening to stand-up comedy podcasts while Kensi slept. He hoped his laughter wouldn't wake her up; she only stirred a little and woke up when they made their first stop for gas and snacks.

"Hey sleepy head. You left me hanging for the last couple of hours. Ready to keep me company now?"

"Eh. Where are we?"

"Mississippi."

"I must have been out for a while. I'll do better the second leg of the trip. Pinky swear."

"Don't make promises you can't keep," Darren said to Kensi's back as she dashed toward the gas station for a restroom break. She despised public restrooms, but had no choice in this situation. This was one of the many reasons she preferred plane rides. She could hold off using the restroom for a few hours. She grabbed a few snacks on the way out to meet her road partner and got comfortable once back inside the car by taking off her shoes and tying her hair back in a ponytail. Much better.

"I grabbed these for you," she said, tossing the candy bars into his lap.

"Thoughtful, check."

"A checklist? Am I passing your tests?"

"Nope. You failed keeping me company. I had to rely on Nephew Tommy and Katt Williams to keep me company."

"Actually, I think I should pass because I'm the one who told you about the comedy stations on Spotify." Kensi made the checkmark motion with her finger.

"Partial check then. You still have time to get full credit," Darren teased and started the engine, returning to the route along I-10 east.

It wasn't long before they made it to Georgia, where they decided to camp out for the night at a local Hampton Inn. They checked into adjoining separate rooms and freshened up for dinner. Darren tried keeping the atmosphere as light as possible along the drive, while still getting to know more about Kensi, but the closeness was beginning to wear on him. The last thing he wanted

Kensi to think was that he was trying to take advantage of her, but it was proving to take more strength than he thought he had to keep his hands to himself. He thought about calling off dinner, giving the excuse that he was tired from the drive. He was tired, but he also needed time to clear his mind so that he wouldn't do anything he'd regret tomorrow morning. As quickly as the thought entered his mind, Kensi knocked on the adjoining door.

Maybe coming along wasn't the best idea, he thought when he opened the door and saw how beautiful Kensi looked in her black cowl-neck sweater and perfect fitting blue jeans. Aside from the gush of cool air coming from her room, her beauty nearly knocked the wind from his chest.

"Ready?"

"Um, I was starting to think that maybe I should stay in and rest. That was a long drive and we're only halfway done," he mustered. He hoped he sounded authentic. Although that was the truth, he needed to be away from her so that his desires wouldn't betray him.

"I guess you're right. I'll order room service so that we can eat in before calling it a night."

"Great idea," Darren agreed. *Bad idea* everything within him screamed, but this time he ignored that little voice and accepted Kensi's invitation to hang out in her room until their food arrived.

Chapter 20

Kensi could hear the voices of her mother and meddlesome aunts floating around in her head, badgering her about Darren and whether or not he was *the one*. Shaking her head as if to rid her mind of those thoughts, she focused on the dinner she was about to have with Darren. He'd been sitting at the desk in her room, flipping through the room service menu. They were both relatively quiet, keeping their attention on the food instead of each other.

After ordering, Kensi sat in the empty chair less than ten feet away from him. There was no denying the tension that was building in that room, and it was starting to become uncomfortable for both of them.

Clearing his throat, Darren asked, "So tell me more about this family of yours. What should I expect?" They hadn't talked about her family in detail before they took the trip. She'd only told him about her cousin who was leaving the country and her parents. She figured if she told him how crazy they all were, he'd probably change his mind and spend Christmas in Pepperton as he'd done for the last few years. But for Darren, crazy wouldn't scare him away. He missed being able to share holidays with family and looked forward to the atmosphere. His father died while on active duty during Darren's junior year in high school. His high school basketball coach always offered a listening ear and stepped in when Darren needed support in his studies. The impact Coach Hawkins had on his life moved him to pursue a career in secondary education. He only hoped that he would impact at least one student's life the way Coach Hawkins impacted his. His mother died one year after he finished college. Jessica had been his rock during that time in his life, and until now, he hadn't had anyone close to him to celebrate the holidays with. He'd take crazy, malfunctioned, uptight, nosey, loving family any day of the year because that's one hundred times better than being without any family.

"Questions. Many many questions! Mostly about your background and your intentions with me. They won't understand that we're only friends. They're gonna want to know when we're getting married and having children. I'm used to the pressure, but don't let them scare you away."

Darren laughed at her response.

"I'm serious Mr. Shaw. I can hear my Mom's voice now. '*A man doesn't just travel across the country all willy nilly with a woman he isn't serious about.*'" Kensi mimicked her mother's voice.

"Sounds about right."

Kensi's features became disapproving with her lips twisted and eyes narrowed. Darren walked over and sat on the floor facing Kensi, resting his elbows on his knees. He grunted a little as he made himself comfortable.

"You're too young for your bones to be cracking like that."

"Maybe. But like I said, your mother is right. We're not serious now, but this thing between us could potentially become serious. I don't just ride across the country with random women. I meant what I said before we finished the production. I'm working on getting to know you. To know us together. To see if we have what it takes for the long haul. Isn't that what you want, too?"

"Yeah, but I just wanted to warn you about all of the questions we'll be facing over the next few days."

"I have no problem sharing my intentions with anyone who asks. I think I've been pretty straightforward about my plans with you, Ms. Jacobson."

"Indeed you have, Mr. Shaw," Kensi agreed and smiled. A wave of relief washed over her at the sound of someone saying "room service" and knocking on the door. Perfect timing in her opinion. Darren was getting serious again, and they needed to keep the moment light. They were closed up in a hotel room for goodness sake. With confessions like that, the mood changes, and anything was bound to happen.

Darren moved to get the door. Kensi remained glued to her seat, but could smell the steak and mahi mahi the moment he opened the door. He tipped the staff, brought the food inside, and set the tray on the table. Both of their stomachs began to growl as he uncovered their dishes. The steak, potatoes, and broccoli on Darren's plate along with Kensi's mahi mahi and steamed mixed vegetables looked just as good as they smelled.

"Let's pray and eat! I think I'm starving now!" Kensi exclaimed.

Darren quickly thanked God for their food before they tore into their entrees. For a moment, there was only the sound of the television playing in the background and the clinking of forks on their plates.

"So are you nervous about taking me home to your family?" Darren asked. Although she invited him, he still sensed a bit of hesitation on her part.

"Not nervous. Just wish I could fast forward through all the questions from them mostly just being nosey."

"We'll be okay. We're grown. We like each other and we want to spend time together. They'll understand," Darren said. He winked and finished off his plate. It took all of ten minutes. Surely he was famished.

Kensi nodded. He didn't know her family like she did, but she'd leave him to see for himself. They were good people; some of them were just a little pushy. She was sure her mom was getting tired of all of her friends showing up with grandbabies and she didn't have any to brag about yet.

Kensi told him a little about her hometown in between bites of food, highlighting the parade and their Christmas family tradition of staying up late in their Christmas-themed pajamas playing board games. That was the one thing she looked forward to. Plain ole family fun.

"I'm looking forward to it," Darren said. He collected their plates and placed the tray outside the door to be picked up by the hotel staff. He stretched and announced that he was calling it a night.

"Me too." Kensi hugged Darren tightly and was starting to feel a bit more relaxed about taking him home to meet her family. She would be surprised if they didn't like him just as much as she did.

"Good night, Ms. Jacobson."

"Good night, Mr. Shaw."

Still standing in his embrace, Kensi lifted her chin and pressed her lips against his. She didn't think much about it; it seemed like the natural thing to do. His lips were warm and inviting as he moved his lips against hers. Darren broke the kiss first. As much as he enjoyed it, he didn't want her to doubt that his intentions were pure.

"I better go while I still have the strength to do so. Sweet dreams. And lock this door behind me so that I can't change my mind and come back for more."

Chapter 21

Darren buzzed Kensi's room around 7 a.m. the next morning to make sure that she was awake and ready for breakfast. After last night's kiss and the dreams he had about the two of them, he wasn't going to risk going anywhere near the adjoining door that connected their rooms. Breakfast was going to have to be in the hotel breakfast area or somewhere out in the open where they wouldn't be alone.

Checking around to make sure they'd grabbed everything, they met in the hallway and walked to the elevator. Thankfully the hotel offered express checkout. Their bills had already been paid, so they didn't have to stop at the front desk.

"What do you want to eat? We can eat inside after getting our bags into the car, or we can stop anywhere you'd like," Darren offered as they stepped off the elevator into the hotel lobby.

"I prefer to keep moving. We can stop at Chick-fil-A for breakfast and continue on our little journey. We still have quite a ways to go."

"As you wish," he said, pushing the door open for her to exit first. The wind nearly knocked her down and she paused in her tracks. It had been warm the day before, and although it wasn't much cooler, she wasn't expecting the gust of wind.

"Hey, are you all right?" Darren asked, placing his right hand in the middle of her back to help her regain balance.

"Yeah," Kensi confirmed after catching her breath. "That just caught me by surprise. That's all."

"Let's roll then."

Darren helped Kensi inside first. After fighting with the wind to put their bags in the trunk, he took a couple of brisk steps to the driver's side of the car and hopped in to find Kensi trying to smooth her hair after being tackled by the strong breeze.

"Almost feels like winter," Darren commented as he started the ignition.

"Not even close."

"We're not going to have a *New York is better* conversation today. No, Ms. Jacobson. Don't even think about it."

"No need. Seems like you've gotten the message already," Kensi pointed out.

They joined hands for a quick prayer asking God to protect them during their travels and headed to Chick-fil-A's drive-thru to buy breakfast.

Neither of them had mentioned the kiss they shared last night. Considering they were still getting to know each other and hadn't established the direction of their relationship or even if they were going to be in a relationship at all, Kensi thought it was something worth talking about, yet she hesitated to bring it up. It meant something, but exactly what, she didn't know.

For the next eight hours, they talked around the kiss they had shared: marriage, family, children, traditions, etc. Nothing about the two of them specifically. Darren thought of bringing it up, but he felt like he'd made himself clear on numerous occasions about where they were headed. Kensi slept for about an hour toward the last leg of the trip, until they were about thirty minutes out from her parents' house.

Kensi had mentioned to her mother that she was bringing Darren, a friend from Pepperton, home with her for Christmas. She had felt at ease with him accompanying her, but all of a sudden, she started feeling nervous. She could feel the speed of her pulse in her hands. She grinned sheepishly and began pointing out landmarks to Darren as they got closer to their destination. Her old high school. The track field where she ran the 400-meter dash. The donut shop she visited nearly every morning before school during her senior year. The bowling alley where she and her friends hung out on the weekends. She noticed other spots where she went out with an old boyfriend, but she didn't want to bring that up. Finally, they pulled into her mom's driveway.

"Ken Ken!" her mother shouted as she flung open the door and ran to the car to greet them.

Was she sitting by the window? Kensi wondered as she stepped out into the warmer than normal evening air and embraced her mother. Darren came around to the passenger side and extended his hand to introduce himself.

"Nonsense! You're family for the next few days. Give me a hug young man!"

"Here we go!" Kensi mouthed to Darren as he hugged her mother. There was no telling how things would end up when this trip was over. Kensi could only pray that her family didn't embarrass her and make it seem as if they were desperately trying to auction her off to be married. She didn't need any help; she was just waiting for the right guy.

"Nice to meet you ma'am!" Darren said, pulling out of the embrace.

"What a fine young man!" Marie spoke loudly, waving to her neighbors, drawing attention to the fact that Kensi brought a man home with her. Miss Susan across the street gave a thumbs up. She just happened to be outside checking her mailbox when they arrived. Kensi's mom was gossipy, so she likely told her that Kensi would be arriving with a man and the exact time she expected them to show up.

Kensi's eyes widened in embarrassment and she left the two of them outside while she went inside to find her father. Her mother probably had the whole neighborhood cheering for her to get married.

The familiar scent of vanilla greeted Kensi as she walked through the house searching for her father. For as long as she could remember, that had always been the scent her mother used to spruce up the house, as she called it. Nothing about their home had changed since she left for college. So many memories came rushing back as she went from room to room.

"Dad! It's so good to see you!" Kensi exclaimed, throwing her arms around her father's neck when she found him sitting in the kitchen gobbling down a bowl of ice cream. At about two hundred fifty pounds, with his cholesterol levels teetering along the high end of the scale, Kensi was certain her mother wouldn't approve of him having dessert at noon, especially before he'd eaten anything of substance. He probably went for it the moment Marie dashed out the door.

"Hey baby girl! Look at you. Just as beautiful as ever. How long are you here?"

"We're here until the day after Shana's wedding."

"We? That's right. There's someone I'm supposed to meet, isn't it? Tell me about him," Charles said, finishing off the bowl of ice cream before Marie returned.

"He's a good man: decent, spiritual, hard-working, family oriented, kind, gentle, and he likes me," Kensi answered her father with a twinkle in her eyes. "And Dad," Kensi added, "please don't let Mom embarrass me."

"Well, y'all *like* each other enough to be taking road trips. Let me go check this fella out." He made no promises to halt Marie from embarrassing her. He scooted away from the table and walked into the living room as Darren was carrying their bags inside, escorted by Marie.

Upon seeing Charles enter the room, Darren extended his hand once again to introduce himself. Charles accepted his handshake and sized him up for a moment, still holding his grasp on Darren's hand. Both Marie and Kensi watched the interaction, waiting on Charles to make the next move. Kensi was starting to feel like she'd invited her prom date over to the house.

"Dad!" she urged.

"Come with me," Charles said to Darren, ignoring Kensi and leading Darren into the kitchen after showing him where to leave their bags.

"Don't look at me. You brought this on yourself. What did you think was going to happen? You haven't been home in over a year and you waltz in here with a man! Take a seat honey. This might take a while," Marie demanded and sat down next to Kensi.

Darren wasn't sure what to expect based on what Kensi shared about her family and the warm welcome he received from her mother. However, he was ready for any question Mr. Jacobson had for him; he had nothing to hide and he cared about Kensi. He had no issues with providing anything short of his social security number if it would help her family feel comfortable with knowing the man after their daughter's heart.

Chapter 22

"This isn't like you . . . traveling across the country with a man. We had to pull teeth to get you to tell us anything about the Adam guy you were dating in New York. You've only known this guy a few weeks and you're already taking road trips. Not typical of the *taking things slow* Kensi that we know. What gives?" her mother probed.

Kensi had proven to be one of the most level-headed persons she knew. She would be the first one shooting fireworks if Kensi was about to settle down soon, but she wondered what made Darren different than anyone else Kensi had dated.

"We're just getting to know each other and this trip happened to be perfect timing. We're taking things slow. And we have to. There would be one huge obstacle in front of us if we decided to take things further," Kensi began opening up to her mother.

"And that is?" Marie questioned, making herself comfortable on the couch as if she was about to hear a juicy story.

"The distance! You know I love New York, and he loves Texas. Neither of us want to move, so there's that."

"The guy obviously has some type of feelings for you or else he wouldn't be traveling across the country with you. But if you two know that's an issue, why even pursue this whole *getting to know each other* business? Why even start something that obviously won't be finished because you two are too selfish to look past what you think you want instead of doing what's best for your relationship to bloom?" she counseled, exaggerating with her arms flailing in the air.

"Of course."

"What? Honey, I've been married for a very long time and you can't get this far without some sort of compromise."

"I know. There could really be something between us and we're not willing to chalk it up because of distance just yet. I guess we're both hoping that the other person would change their mind, give in and move to another state."

While Marie continued to advise Kensi in the love department, Charles was in the kitchen getting the 4-1-1 on Darren.

He sat in the kitchen with his laptop open performing a background check. Aside from google, he had access to a service they used at church to perform background checks on volunteers before they served with the children or the finance ministry. At this point, Darren wondered if Charles was going to ask for his fingerprints. Definitely not what Darren expected.

Once he cleared, Charles began questioning him about his intentions with his daughter. He had no doubt that Darren was smitten with his Kensi, but he was curious as to why he'd travel with her without any sort of commitment.

"Just what exactly are you two doing? What are your plans?" Charles questioned.

"Kensi is near perfect for me, but I don't know if she's ready to commit to a relationship given that she has to return to - New York soon. And I don't know if starting a long-distance relationship is the best move for us." Charles mirrored the exact sentiments that his wife shared with Kensi: If this thing wasn't going anywhere, why even start?

"But I think we can manage to make it work if we can agree that we want to be together."

"Whatever you do, don't break her heart. She may be a grown woman, but she is still my daughter. You understand that, don't ya?"

"Yes sir."

The conversation shifted to Darren's holiday traditions and what he usually did around that time. During his background check, Charles found out about Darren's previous marriage, so Darren discussed what he did with Jessica and what he used to do as a child. He didn't want to withhold any information from her father. He didn't need him to suspect that he was deceitful.

Charles closed the lid to the laptop, leaned back in his chair and folded his arms across his chest, eyeing Darren skeptically. "Are you sure you're ready to move forward? I don't want Kensi to get caught up with you only for you to realize that you're not ready for a relationship because of unresolved issues you have surrounding the passing of Jessica."

"I understand sir, but Kensi doesn't have to worry about that. I'm ready. Spending time with Kensi has actually proven to me that it's possible to love again, completely."

"I see . . . well, you're welcome to spend Christmas with our family. Just make sure you stay in the guest bedroom."

He was grateful that her parents welcomed him. Their stamp of approval was the biggest hurdle in his mind and her father had just given it to him. Although meeting the parents didn't usually come until much later, he was glad that he'd gotten the chance to do it sooner.

After chatter about sports, the men joined Marie and Kensi in the living room to find them putting up the Christmas tree.

When Marie learned that Kensi, her only child, would be home for Christmas, she decided to save that task so that she and Kensi could do it together. She wanted to reminisce over old times and when ornaments were collected over the years. It warmed her heart that Kensi was home. The only thing that would warm her heart even more was grandbabies, but she wouldn't bring that up just yet.

"Can we help?" Darren asked.

"Sure, grab a string of lights," Marie instructed.

Marie told the story of Kensi shaking the Christmas tree when she was a child, causing the tree to fall over. Luckily, her dad was only a few steps away to catch the tree before it fell on top of her. She'd been trying to reach a candy cane that was placed on the top half of the tree.

"Poor thing. It frightened her to death. I didn't think she'd ever want to look at a Christmas tree again, but she surprised me. It was the one thing she looked forward to every Christmas, besides the presents."

Kensi and Darren talked about the assignment in Pepperton and how they celebrated Christmas there.

"You'll have to come visit some time. It's probably one of the nicest small-town Christmas experiences you'll ever have."

"Umm, I'm still waiting for them to visit me, so you must know that they'll be coming to New York before they go to Pepperton," Kensi added.

"We'll see about that, won't we?" Darren said and smiled.

Marie and Charles exchanged looks, but didn't say anything, which was out of the ordinary for Marie, who seemed to have a comment about everything.

"Well Darren, I'm sure Kensi explained to you how we get down on Christmas Eve! The pizza and the rest of the family will be here shortly. It's time to change into your pajamas and get ready for family game night. I hope you're good, or else I surely don't want any losers my team!" Marie exclaimed.

"Yes ma'am."

Kensi led Darren back down the long hallway that Charles had previously led him down to put away their things.

"The bathroom is the second door to the right," she pointed out.

He grabbed both of her hands and said, "Thank you for letting me tag along. Feels like family."

"No problem, but don't thank me just yet. You haven't met everyone," Kensi said and laughed.

"I'm not worried because I'm exactly where I need to be." Darren squeezed her hands tightly before leaving her side to freshen up. At that moment, his heart and mind were on the same page. He was ready to take the next step with Kensi. He just hoped that she was ready as well.

Chapter 23

"Here comes the bride!" Marie sang as she swung open the door for Shana and Eric. Shana, Kensi's cousin, was just as loud, lively and intrusive as Marie, the complete opposite of her fiancé, Eric. Whenever he attended one of their family functions, he'd spend a few moments catching up, grab his plate of food, and go off to connect with any male cousins or uncles who were present. He knew that whenever Shana linked up with her family, it would be like watching a TV sitcom, so he'd relax and enjoy the show. And tonight, wasn't any different because the moment he and Shana stepped through the door and greeted Kensi's parents with hugs, she left his side and made a beeline to Kensi and Darren, who stood to hug them as well.

"The beautiful bride!" Kensi squealed.

"Kensi!" Shana threw her arms around Kensi's neck and squeezed her for several seconds, whispering in her ear, "I miss you girl! You do know I'm 'bout to screen him, right?"

She finally withdrew from the embrace to introduce her fiancé. "Honey, this is Darren Shaw. And you remember Kensi." Eric moved to Virginia during Shana and Kensi's senior year in high school, though he and Shana didn't start dating until about five years ago.

"Nice to meet you man." Eric and Darren shook hands and embraced with their free hand.

"Same here, and congratulations on your upcoming nuptials."

"Thanks man, I appreciate that."

Kensi hugged Eric. "Congratulations again! I'm happy for you guys! I'm surprised this woman hasn't driven you crazy yet."

"Only in the best way," Eric answered.

"Umm hmm. You can tell me the truth later," Kensi pretended to be skeptical. Shana led Darren back to the sofa and took the reins of the conversation, directing her attention to the newcomer, while Eric took a seat to the other side of her, leaving Kensi to find a seat elsewhere.

"Darren! I have heard *so* much about you, I almost feel like I know you already," she said, winking at Kensi. Shana hustled out of her jacket to sit down beside Darren.

"Is that right?"

"Umm hmm. So you have the hots for my cousin, huh?"

"Shana!" Kensi admonished.

Without even looking in Kensi's direction, she waved her off, keeping her eyes glued on Darren, her smile spread across her face. Being all up in Kensi's business was right up her alley. She'd been waiting on this moment since she first heard of Kensi being on a date with Darren.

"Don't say that too loud. It might go to her head," Darren said, egging Shana on.

"I would ask you to tell me about yourself, but I think I know just about everything about you from where you work, where you're from, what you like to do, how spiritual you are, your favorite food, the type of cologne you wear and how it meshes well with your body chemistry," Shana counted off on her fingertips.

Kensi loudly cleared her throat. If her parents hadn't embarrassed her enough, she was surely mortified now. The poor guy was probably going to think that she was obsessed with him, the way Shana was carrying on.

"That sound meant that I need to straighten up and that Kensi didn't really tell me all those things about you, right Kensi?" Shana teased in a much lower voice. Eric also nudged her and mouthed *take it easy*.

"Game time! We can get started before Auntie Doty and the rest of the cousins get here. Good idea? Great!" Kensi exclaimed, not waiting on anyone to agree with her. She pulled out the newest version of the Bop It game and explained the rules. Although having a family game night on Christmas Eve was the reason they were gathered, no one moved a muscle to begin playing the game.

"Let's at least wait for the pizza, Ken Ken!" Marie chimed in. "You can bake cookies and check on my special hot chocolate that's brewing in the crockpot if you need to get out of here."

Marie was not making the situation any better, but Kensi accepted the task and the opportunity to leave the room. She went to check on the hot chocolate and put the turtle chocolate chip cookies in the oven. She could feel heat rising on the back of her neck from embarrassment.

Popping balls of dough onto the cookie sheet, she inwardly chastised herself for bringing Darren home, especially since she hadn't been home in a while. Her family needed to be prepped first—not that it would have mattered anyway. The more she thought about it, the more she realized that this whole scenario would have likely played out the same way whenever she brought him or anyone else home.

"Need any help?" Darren asked, walking into the kitchen dressed in his plaid red and green pajamas with Rudolph the red-nosed reindeer house shoes that matched her own. Getting matching house shoes was his idea.

"Umm, sure."

Darren washed his hands, went to Kensi's side and helped place cookie dough on the cookie sheet.

"You okay?"

"Yeah . . . I told you they were crazy. Tried to warn you," Kensi sang.

"Sounds like you're more worried about that than I am. They're your family and I'm sure they're only looking out for you. Besides, I can tell that Shana acts like that because she knows it gets to you. Your reaction is reason for her to keep going. I like her though. She's funny."

"Just blending right on in, I see," she commented, pausing to squint her eyes at him.

"What?"

"You just might belong on the crazy train with all of them."

"If being on that train means that I care about you, then I'm all aboard."

Knowing that her family's antics weren't running him away gave her some sort of relief, although she almost wanted to run away herself. She expected it, but hadn't known to what extent it would come.

Darren walked over to the crockpot and lifted the lid. "This smells really good. What's in it?"

"I don't really know. She won't share it with us, but I'm sure it's something she found on Pinterest. It's really good though. It should be about ready. Want to try it?"

"Sure."

Kensi pulled out two mugs from the cupboard and served hot cocoa for the two of them while Darren put the cookies in the preheated oven. Since it seemed that the family had forgotten about them for a while and refocused their attention to Shana's wedding, Darren and Kensi took a seat at the breakfast nook, wrapping their hands around the warm mugs, and enjoyed the brief time alone. The sounds of holiday music were now playing through the stereo speakers in the living room, so Darren and Kensi hoped they could have a semi-private moment.

Darren sipped his cocoa and agreed that it was very good. He sat for a moment trying to figure out the flavors that were mixed in with the cocoa, but couldn't put his fingers on it.

"Are you comfortable enough with me to date exclusively?" Darren asked. He pushed a stray hair behind her ear and eyed her intently, waiting patiently for her to answer.

"Before I answer that, tell me you're not only asking me that because you're feeling pressured by my family."

"Definitely not. We agreed to spend time getting to know each other and we're doing that. I like what I'm seeing and I want to make a go of it." He spoke confidently, but softly to keep that conversation between the two of them.

"Then I am too. But are you sure you want to do the long-distance thing? You know I have to go back to New York after the New Year, right?"

"I'm aware of that, but if we both want this, can't we try to make it work?"

"Welcome aboard the train, Mr. Shaw."

Darren chuckled and tilted his mug toward hers. This would have been the perfect moment to seal the deal with a kiss, but that would have to wait until some other time considering they were in her parents' home. That was one more thing they had to look forward to, but for now, they would rejoin the family for pizza, games, cookies, and questions about the status of their relationship.

Chapter 24

Kensi and Darren entered the family room carrying a tray of assorted chocolate chip cookies and mugs of peppermint cocoa for everyone. The pizzas had already arrived, so they made room on the table next to the stack of pizzas and got comfortable on the sofa.

The room fell silent when the two of them entered, leading them to believe they were the topic of conversation while they were in the kitchen. Kensi hated the awkward feeling that washed over her. Her family had to make this a spectacle. Why couldn't they behave normally for one moment?

The family's eyes were glued on Kensi and Darren as if they were waiting for some sort of an explanation, but neither of them offered anything.

"So, were we holding you guys up from eating?" Kensi asked. The silence was starting to become a little weird. The only sound was the Christmas carols playing softly on the TV music station. If they were the type of family who quietly sat around listening to music, she wouldn't see a problem, but they were far from quiet at any given time, other than when they were sleeping.

"You tell me!" Marie all but screamed, her tone holding a hint of suspicion.

"We're all good. Right?" she asked Darren. Everyone's eyes then shifted to him as he nodded in agreement.

"Party time!" Shana jumped in. She hoped Kensi didn't think she was going to be coming to her rescue all night; she was in the hotspot and she knew it.

As if Shana was the referee, the family broke their silence and resumed chatting, grabbing pizza and cookies and settling into their blankets that covered the carpeted floor to play their first game of the night—Monopoly. The next couple of hours were filled with shouts of *you landed on my property, pay up, throw me the dice, pass me a chance card,* and sighs of relief for passing *Go.* Shana was the last player standing and made sure to gloat about her win.

After a couple of hours of playing Monopoly, they played Uno, Phase 10, Twister, Taboo and ended with a checkers tournament. Kensi had missed spending time with her family like this. She couldn't believe that she'd allowed the family pressures to get married to keep her away. Darren couldn't remember the last time he'd had so much fun enjoying family. Although he'd come to accompany Kensi, he probably needed this trip much more than he thought.

Marie and Darren were the last standing in the checkers tournament. Everyone else other than Shana and Kensi had fallen asleep or was beginning to nod off.

"Are you enjoying yourself, young man?" Marie asked. She was up against Darren in the tournament. Though she was trying to distract him a little, she really wanted to know if he was having a good time.

"Yes ma'am. Probably one of the best Christmases I've had in a very long time."

"Well, we'll just have to invite you back next year then!"

"And I'd be happy to come along."

"King me, king me, king me!" Marie taunted.

Darren chuckled and added a black checkered chip on top of another of her checkers that made it across the board. He should have seen that coming. The friendly chatter was a trick. That was the first time during the game that she'd been friendly.

Kensi and Shana had stopped playing a while ago because they were caught up chitchatting. They'd started cleaning the living room by throwing away pizza boxes and loading mugs into the dishwasher.

"He seems nice, Kens. I like him for you!" Shana commented. After closing the dishwasher, she embraced her cousin.

"Goodness girl! I miss this! It is so good to see you."

"I know! I'm going to miss you even more now that you're moving across the ocean. Don't you take too long getting back over here to us. Okay, so wedding. Day after Christmas. What do you need me to do?"

Shana and Kensi sat down at the kitchen table, chatting like it was 2 p.m. instead of 2 a.m. They were planning to keep things simple by having a boutique wedding at the church with family and a few close friends, followed by a reception in the fellowship hall. Shana pulled out her notebook and checklist. Everything had been taken care of already. All she needed was for Kensi to stand next to her on her special day. She handed the checklist to Kensi to look over and make sure she wasn't forgetting anything.

"Looks good to me. How did you get them to agree to cater your reception the day after Christmas?" Kensi asked, referring to a few of the older women on the Mother's Board.

"Honey, money talks! Now . . . all of my stuff is taken care of. What are you and Darren going to do?" Shana asked, closing the binder and redirecting Kensi's attention to her own situation.

"It's a done deal. We're going to see where this leads us."

Shana squealed. She was probably more excited for Kensi than Kensi was for herself. Now that she was getting married, Shana wanted nothing more but for Kensi to experience the same happiness.

After agreeing to call it a night, Kensi dug her cellphone out of her purse and placed it on the charger. She hadn't checked it since she arrived, figuring that no one would be contacting her during this time, and if they did, surely it could wait until after the holidays.

She had eight missed calls from Samantha and five from Adam. Nothing about that could be good, she thought. The better part of her wanted to ignore the calls and voicemails until after the holidays, but she wouldn't be able to enjoy her family if she did that. She couldn't believe she was checking voicemails at 2:30 a.m. After listening to the messages, one in particular from Samantha caused a lump to form in her throat and uncertainty to creep back into her heart.

"Kensi, I have great news for you! I wish I could have delivered this news to you over the phone instead of through a voicemail, but we've decided that it would be a great idea to have

two assistant editor-in-chief positions. Congratulations, you'll be working alongside Adam! We can work things out with the Pepperton Quad since you're rolling off of your temporary assignment. Please make arrangements to return to the office next week! Call me if you have any questions."

"Why are you looking like a deer caught in headlights?"

Kensi moved robotically to the counter and plugged her phone into the charger. Her voice matched her movement. "Shana, they're giving me the job now. I got the promotion. They want me back in New York next week." Her hands trembled as she folded her arms across her chest.

"Congratulations!" Shana squealed and nearly knocked Kensi over as she threw her arms around her neck. When she realized that Kensi wasn't returning the hug, she broke the embrace and asked, "This is what you wanted, isn't it? Wait—you don't seem too happy about it."

"That's because I don't know if I am."

Chapter 25

Christmas morning should have been filled with joy and expectation, but instead Kensi was confused and uncertain. She'd finally come to terms with the fact that Samantha passed over her and gave her dream job to Adam in spite of his lack of qualification to preserve her legacy, and now the job was being dropped in her lap. Three months ago she would have jumped at the opportunity, but now she wasn't so sure it was the right choice.

She mulled over the messages while brushing her teeth for at least fifteen minutes. She spent twice as much time getting dressed for church service; her cousin and mother had come by to check on her twice. She made an extra effort to sound cheerful behind the closed doors, but that was the last word she would use to describe how she was feeling.

Although she knew she would have to go back to New York, the new position somehow changed things for her. What did this mean for her new relationship with Darren? She wasn't sure, but she didn't have peace when thinking about any of it. Not the kind of peace she believed she should have when God presented an opportunity to her. What happened to the truth behind Proverbs 10:22 that says, "The blessing of the Lord makes one rich, and He adds no sorrow to it?" Hopefully she'd get some clarity during service today. That always seemed to help.

Kensi emerged from her childhood bedroom where the walls were still covered in pink and white stripes. She was surprised that her mother hadn't changed it since she'd been away for nearly fifteen years. The floors creaked under her feet, alerting the family that she was coming down the hallway.

"Welcome to the land of the living!" Marie greeted Kensi when she joined the family in the living room.

"Good morning, Momma," Kensi said and kissed Marie's cheeks. "I'm ready."

A resounding "Merry Christmas" came from everyone else in the room.

"Merry Christmas! You're beautiful."

"Thank you." Kensi blushed at the sentiment. And for a moment, her worries went away. Back was the joy of Christmas and all of the love and peace that came along with it.

Marie, Charles and two of Kensi's aunts loaded up in one car while Kensi and Darren got in the car with Shana and her fiancé. Kensi was hoping for a moment alone with Darren to tell him about the promotion, but now that had to wait. She thought that should be a private conversation, given their circumstances.

The church was a five-minute drive away from Kensi's parents' home. Just as quickly as they were in the cars, they were all getting out and joining each other in front of the church entrance. The weather was cool, but not like Kensi would have liked. She preferred a white Christmas, with just enough snow covering the ground that it would melt overnight. Every now and again they'd see it there, but this didn't seem to be one of those years.

Kensi gave Darren's hand a reassuring squeeze before they entered the doors of the church. He smiled as they walked inside. A small family church. This had been what he'd grown accustomed to in Pepperton. Although everyone seemed to know everything about everybody, he loved the close-knit community that came with belonging to a small church. That reminded him that he'd probably be receiving a few text messages and calls later from church members who didn't see him in the service this morning. He smiled at the thought.

On their way to their seats, Marie made it her business to introduce Darren to as many people as she could before service started. She'd grown tired of other women in the church throwing their sons-in-law and grandbabies in her face. She had to let them know that she'd soon have pictures and grandbabies to show off as well. Although Kensi and Darren weren't even close to getting married, in her mind they may as well have been. Darren was handsome, treated her daughter well, and as far as she was concerned, part of their family already. This time next year, she'd be planning her daughter's wedding for sure.

Darren took it all in stride, smiling, shaking hands and passing out hugs. Besides, he found Marie loving, yet entertaining. She all but said he was engaged to her daughter. Anyone halfway listening would have inferred that from her conversation.

"The way things are going, folks around here are going to expect you to have a ring on your finger the next time you come home," Darren whispered in Kensi's ear when he finally sat down next to her.

"I told you she was ruthless," Kensi said, using an *I told you so* tone.

"She has good intentions . . . to see her daughter happy and to fill her house with grandchildren. I can respect that."

"Yea, but she needs to work on her delivery," Kensi responded. Her neck was starting to grow warm. Something about Darren's last statement made her a little nervous. He was becoming one of *them*. Her family was transforming him in front of her eyes, unless that's who he had been all along.

"Maybe. I guess it's just that you have everything else. She sees it as the next natural step for you. That's all."

Yea, I do too, but I'm not carrying on like that.

They stood as instructed to sing along with the choir, participate in the responsive reading and offering. The pastor's message was brief, but he spoke about the birth of Jesus Christ and the hope that came along with Jesus' birth. The message that Kensi got from the pastor's sermon was that God sometimes does things in unconventional ways. What doesn't make sense to us makes sense to God because He can see the bigger picture. Of course her current situation lay heavily on her heart as she thought about the lesson.

Only God knew what was best and this job had been what she wanted. Maybe she had needed to grow or learn a lesson before she could have it? She wasn't sure, but she did know that she couldn't turn it down, hence the reason she sent an e-mail to Samantha when she arrived back at her parents' home wishing her a Merry Christmas and accepting the assistant editor-in-chief role. She had to find out if it was everything she dreamed it would be and she had to prove to Samantha that she was the best person for the position all along.

Chapter 26

The dinner table was covered with ham, turkey, dressing, mustard greens, macaroni and cheese, sweet potatoes, green bean casserole, and an assortment of cakes and pies. About five different conversations were taking place as the Jacobson family enjoyed their Christmas dinner. Coupled with the Christmas music playing on the TV music station, the atmosphere was lively and especially loud with conversations and laughter.

"Now Kensi," Marie said as she took the floor, "You better stop pussyfootin' around and hook Darren while you can. I saw a couple of those fast thangs from church eyeballing him during service this morning! Hmph."

"Really Momma?!" Kensi was hoping that they'd moved past this.

"Yes, really! I know a good man when I see one," Marie continued on with the rest of the family encouraging her with their *"yep," "that's right," and" "tell her, Marie"* statements.

"I'll be sure to keep that in mind, Momma," Kensi said, hoping to stop the conversation.

"You saw them, didn't you Darren? Especially that thang with the too tight red dress on . . . just no respect for herself."

"No ma'am. I was focused on the sermon, and a little on Kensi to be honest."

Kensi blushed at Darren's comment. Part of her couldn't wait for this to be over, because they weren't going to let her live it down and it seemed as if Darren would continue playing into Marie's agenda.

"See there! Hey hey! Look at that!" Marie shouted, directing everyone's attention to the two of them. If anyone wasn't paying attention before, they were now.

"We get it, dearest Mother. Let's have some dessert now, shall we?" Kensi asked, a little more formal than needed. Her eyes pleaded with Marie to stop, and to her surprise, she dropped the subject for the time being.

After dessert, the family shuffled into the living room and sat near the tree as Marie pulled each gift from under the tree, read the gift tag and handed the package to the recipient. While everyone was busy ripping the wrapping paper from boxes and tearing through gift bags, Darren handed a small box to Kensi. The gesture did not go unnoticed by Marie, who dramatically clutched her chest and stood with her mouth opened wide. He'd given her a beautiful pair of earrings, with a stone the color of her birthstone. Marie visibly and audibly exhaled since she'd been holding her breath. She wasn't sure why she thought it would be a ring, since Darren and Kensi had only met about a month before. But she couldn't help but hold out hope that the time had come.

"These are beautiful."

"Like the new owner. When you wear your hair in a ponytail, I never see you wearing earrings. When I saw these, I thought they were perfect for you."

"They are. I love them," Kensi thanked Darren and leaned to place a quick peck on his cheek.

He opened his gift from her. Inside his box was a light blue polo shirt and a beautiful wood framed picture of them at the ice skating rink on their first date.

"Thank you for thinking of me," he said.

"Of course, and just so you know, I put that picture in there so that you won't forget me when I move back to New York,"

Kensi said, running her fingers along the word "Houston" that was engraved all over the wood. Her voice trailed off to a whisper as she choked back the tears and emotion.

"Never that."

"We need to talk. Let's go for a walk so that we can have a little privacy."

Darren accepted Kensi's invitation and they moved to get their coats, stepping over empty boxes and wrapping paper. He helped her into her coat and then slid into his, covering his head with a black knitted cap.

Stepping outside of the house was refreshing and peaceful. The never-ending chatter and music could be draining. With Darren grabbing hold of Kensi's hand, they started down the driveway, passing Marie's empty rosebushes, and began their trail on the sidewalk. For a moment, they simply enjoyed the peacefulness that came with being outside the house and the Christmas decorations and lights that adorned several of the homeowners' landscape.

"I got some news a couple of nights ago. It looks like you have to go back to Texas without me. They're giving me the promotion and they want me back next week," Kensi blurted out. She was happy to get it off her chest, but unsure of how Darren would take the news.

"Congratulations," was all he said at first. He knew that was what Kensi had her heart set on for a while, but in the back of his mind, he'd hoped that she'd come to Pepperton to stay, regardless of the number of times she voiced that she would never move there.

"Is that all?"

"It's what you've wanted for a very long time. I'm happy for you. Was I hoping that we'd get to spend a little more time together? Sure, but I'll never attempt to stand in the way of you following any dreams you have. I'm here to support you."

Relief washed over Kensi, knowing that Darren didn't have any ill feelings. It wasn't like neither of them knew this was coming. She had to return to New York sooner or later.

"I know. I'm sorry to drop the news on you like this."

He stopped walking and grabbed her other hand so that they were face to face. "Never apologize for pursuing your dreams. You had that dream long before you met me, and it's like we agreed, we believe we have something going here, so we'll try and work it out as best we can, right?"

"Right." Kensi leaned forward to kiss Darren for being so understanding and even more attractive to her at that very moment.

In the distance, they heard yelling and turned to see Marie and Shana standing on the sidewalk in front of her parents' lawn, cheering.

"She will not stop embarrassing me, I see."

"She's only doing it because she knows it gets to you . . . just like Shana. C'mon let's get back and enjoy the rest of the time we have together. We can talk later," Darren suggested.

They slowly walked back toward her parents' house while Kensi made every effort to shoo them back inside. Kensi was glad that things seemed to be falling into place for her, though she hoped that she and Darren would be able to work out a compromise on where they would live, because she wasn't quite sold on becoming a small-town girl just yet.

Chapter 27

Today was all about Shana. Kensi woke up the morning after Christmas excited, anticipating the love and togetherness the day would bring. This would be one of the days she and Shana dreamt about when they were younger, so she looked forward to being a part of Shana's dreams coming true. And for once, the attention would be off her marital status and the aging of her ovaries.

Kensi, Shana, Marie, Ruby, and the rest of the aunts left the men at home and went out to get manicures and pedicures for Shana's wedding that afternoon. It was the day after Christmas and the temperature was twenty-five degrees warmer than the day before. That made for a beautiful day to get married. Shana didn't think about the weather when she chose her wedding gown, she just went with the most beautiful dress that accentuated her curves, and that happened to be a sweetheart mermaid dress.

When they arrived at the church to help Shana get ready, her mother helped with her makeup and hair. Giving their sentiments, her mother first pinned a small broach in the middle of her bra—*something old.* Kensi pinned a pearl-studded hairpin in her hair—*something new.* Marie clasped her pearls around Shana's neck—*something borrowed.* Her garter belt was her *something blue.*

"You look beautiful today, baby. Momma is so proud of you. We're surely going to miss you," Ruby cried.

Shana wiped the tears that were smudging her mother's makeup. She pursed her lips together and inhaled deeply to keep from becoming too emotional and ruining her own makeup. Shana hadn't thought much about the fact that she was about to get married and whisk away to South Africa for a while. She'd be experiencing much of the next several months without her family, but she was charged with *leaving and cleaving*, so she figured she better get used to that.

"It's okay, Momma. We'll miss you too, but I taught you how to use Marco Polo, skype, and video chat with me through Google hangouts, so it'll feel like I'm right here."

"You just don't go having any babies while you're over there. You hear me?" her mother carried on as if Shana was getting ready to board the plane any second.

"C'mon now, Ruby, let the girl enjoy the day! You're about to bring me down," Marie blurted out. "Now twirl around and let Aunt Marie look at you!"

Shana slid her fingers through the loop of the train and shimmied around in a circle to show off her final look. From the pearl-studded hairpin securing her curls down to her French manicured toes, she was stunning. The pearl-studded beads that accented the back of the dress were the perfect touch.

"You look flawless! Eric is one lucky man!" Kensi chimed in.

"Lucky? Pssh! Honey, I'm his favor!" Shana countered, and winked at Kensi.

"I'm so happy for you," Kensi shrieked, wrapping her arms around Shana and squeezing tight, making a special effort not to touch her makeup or hair.

The First Lady's knock on the bride's holding room door alerted them that the time had come.

"Are we ready in here?" she asked, after complimenting Shana.

Shana nodded and turned to watch her wedding from the window. She could see them, but they couldn't see her. She smiled when she saw Eric standing next to the pastor, waiting for her to enter. Her heart began beating triple time as the moment drew closer to make her entrance. The seating of their mothers, the singing of *Center of My Joy*, and the processional of her flower girl and maid of honor, Kensi, all seemed to move a lot quicker than she thought it would. The next thing she knew, it was time for her to meet Eric at the altar. For a moment, she felt sad. She wished that her father had lived to walk her down the aisle, but she found joy in the fact that he would have been proud of her choice.

She glided down the aisle to the melody of How Deeply I Need You, holding a bouquet of white lilies. The guests consisted of their immediate families and their closest friends. She walked slowly, purposely posing for pictures, causing the guests to chuckle. She wanted to help her photographer get the best shots of her.

When she made it to the end of the aisle, her mother stood when the pastor asked who was giving her away. Ruby placed Shana's hands in Eric's and squeezed the two of them together, said a quick prayer and moved to take her seat.

They stood facing each other, hand in hand, as the pastor started officiating. Though she enjoyed the ceremony, it all seemed to move too quickly for Shana. They lit the unity candle, said their vows, exchanged rings, jumped the broom, and the next moment, they were being announced as husband and wife.

Though it wasn't her day, something about it left Kensi anxious. She purposely avoided eye contact with Darren during the ceremony. She wasn't sure why. Maybe it was because weddings tended to make people think about the next steps in their own lives. Or maybe because she was the only single woman in the church. Or it could be that she didn't want Darren to think that she wanted to be next, although she did. She didn't want to make him feel awkward.

The wedding party stayed behind for photos as the rest of the guests, except Darren, moved to the fellowship hall for the reception. He didn't miss the fact that she hadn't looked at him for longer than two seconds since the wedding started. He was aware of her feelings about her family's pressures on her to get married, and he wanted to make sure that she was all right. However, it was hard to read her since she wouldn't even make eye contact with him.

"Darren, come get in these pictures!" Shana called to him. Kensi's eyes grew wide as Shana waved him over, but she didn't say anything. It was Shana's wedding and Shana's photos, so she could have any person in the pictures that she wanted. "Stand beside Kensi," she directed.

Darren didn't waste a second moving as instructed. He placed his hand above Kensi's waist and smiled for the camera.

After several shots, the photographer dismissed everyone but the bride and groom. Darren engulfed her hand in his as they trailed behind the rest of the party.

"Are you okay?"

"Of course. I'm excited for Shana! One of her dreams came true today. Why do you ask?"

"Just checking on you…there's a lot going on."

"Yeah but I'm just focused on making sure the bride is good. Maid of honor duties and such."

"I see." Darren thought to ask if she was sure, but dropped the issue.

They walked through the breezeway that connected the church to the fellowship hall. Unfortunately, there was no breeze today. It was easily eighty degrees, at least that's what it felt like.

The fellowship hall was decorated with pink and green tablecloths on five tables, and black and gold tablecloths on the other five tables to represent the bride and groom's favorite colors. The guests had already begun making moves on the dance floor to the latest party songs. Instead of finding a seat, Darren surprised himself and asked Kensi to dance with him.

Kensi and Darren had only gotten a chance to dance to one song before the bride and groom arrived. They wasted no time continuing the festivities with their first dance. When Luther

Vandross' *Here and Now* ended, Eric pulled a chair to the center of the floor and helped Shana sit. He creatively pulled her garter belt down and off and stood, helping her out of the chair. Marie handed her the bouquet and the microphone.

"Will Kensi and Darren please join us?" Shana asked, a huge smile spread across her face.

"Oh goodness . . . just when I thought it was over," Kensi mumbled, but obliged Shana's request.

"It's all in fun; let's just enjoy it," Darren encouraged. He and Kensi met the newlywed couple on the dance floor, with Darren leading. He could feel the resistance as he held Kensi's hand, almost pulling her along.

"There's no need to toss the bouquet or garter belt since you two are the only single souls at this shindig, so we're just gonna give them to you all." Shana winked at Kensi while Eric patted Darren's back on their way to their seats. Shana twirled her finger in the air at the DJ, indicating that he could start the music again for the two. He played Brian McKnight's *Still in Love*. Darren bowed and pulled Kensi closer to him for their dance.

"See, this isn't so bad, is it?" Darren asked. "You smell great. I love that scent you're wearing."

"Thank you. . . . This is just a teensy bit embarrassing, that's all."

"Lighten up. We're all family here. I'm sure it could be worse, right?" Darren chuckled a bit.

"You're one of them now, I see. I'm glad you're enjoying this."

"Enjoying spending this time with you, yes I am. Thanks for inviting me. No Christmas in Pepperton could have topped this!" He added, when he noticed she couldn't stop looking around at the guests, "Hey, don't worry about them. Let's just enjoy this moment—this dance," he said softly, holding her gently as they swayed to the music.

Kensi started to relax in his arms. They hadn't really been that close before, except for the kiss back in Georgia. And she had to admit to herself that she was really enjoying it.

With their time together coming to an end in less than twenty-four hours, she wasn't sure how they would make their relationship work with her being all the way in New York and him being back in Texas. More and more, she was starting to get used to him being around. How were they going to maintain their growth in two different parts of the country? She didn't have the answers, but she was certain she didn't want to keep up a long-distance relationship for too long. Someone had to give in.

Chapter 28

Kensi awakened to the smell and sizzle of bacon, which reminded her of Saturdays growing up in her parents' home. First, a huge breakfast and then on to Saturday chores followed by shopping. She stretched, hopped out of bed, freshened up, and quickly dressed so that she could meet her mom in the kitchen and help out if possible. It was also her last day in town and she wanted to make the best of it. She couldn't imagine how things were going to go when she returned to New York, so it could very well be this time next year before she got a chance to visit her parents again.

"Good morning," Darren greeted Kensi when she bumped into him, rushing out of her room. He reached out to steady her and pulled her into his arms for a quick embrace.

"Umm. Good morning to you. How did you sleep?"

"Not bad. The crickets put me to sleep and the birds woke me up."

"Don't act like you're not used to that in Pepperton."

"Am not. But yours being the first face I see this morning makes it all better."

Kensi returned his compliment with a peck on the cheek and locked her fingers in his as they walked into the kitchen.

"It smells like 1995 in this kitchen. Can I help you with something, Mom?"

"You all just have a seat and let me serve you one last time before you get on the road." Her voice was softer than it had been since they got there a few days ago.

"Thanks Momma."

"Thanks Mrs. Jacobson."

Marie shuffled around the kitchen finishing up the Belgian waffles, scrambled eggs, grits, bacon, and biscuits. As she prepared the plates, she yelled for Charles to join them in the kitchen. For a moment, Kensi thought they would ambush her again about her personal life, but she decided she wouldn't let that bother her. That was just how they were and it didn't seem like they were going to change anytime soon, so she'd suck it up.

"Charles, lead us in prayer," Marie said, extending her hands to either side of her, causing everyone else to do the same, so they would all be connected. Charles went beyond asking God to bless their food and prayed for Kensi and Darren's travel safety, God's guidance for their lives, and that they'd grow closer to Him. A resounding Amen rung around the table when he finished praying as they prepared to eat.

"What time do your flights leave?" Charles started the conversation.

"We both have 5:30 departures," Darren answered in between bites. Kensi nodded in agreement.

Kensi's return to New York earlier than expected cancelled their road trip back to Pepperton. Darren would return the rental car at the airport and they'd go their separate ways.

"So how are you two planning to make this work?" Marie asked, wagging her fork.

"Everything will be the same, Momma. We just won't see each other every day, at least not in person. There are tons of phone apps that will keep us visually connected."

"You young folks are killing me with these phones and technology. We didn't have all of that back in my day. If you were in a relationship, the man courted the woman until they got married. How are y'all gonna get to the next step being on opposite sides of the country?" Marie countered, her voice raising a few octaves. One would think that they were standing across the room as loud as her voice was. She was back to herself. When she was standing at the stove a while ago, she must not have had her coffee yet. She was usually up and ready to roll after a few sips.

"Well Momma, to be fair, that's all we have. We'll take trips to see each other when we can and try to stay connected as much as possible. Right?"

"Yes ma'am. We have a strong connection, so we're gonna do all we can to make it work."

"Umm hmm," Marie grunted before lifting her coffee mug to her lips. She nudged Charles with her elbow, hoping that he would jump in, but he didn't have anything to add that they didn't already consider.

"It will work as long as you both want it to work. The key is that you both have to want it," he added. He wasn't sure what Marie wanted him to say. Tell Kensi to move to Texas? Encourage Darren to move to New York? Those were the only two options other than what they'd planned to do. And in his opinion, one of them moving wasn't a good idea if they weren't engaged or nearing that step. He would never suggest that his daughter pack up her life without any sort of commitment from Darren, or anyone else for that matter.

"Thanks Mr. Jacobson. That is what we both want."

Marie wasn't trying to rush them into anything, but she was more than ready for a house full of grandchildren. In her mind, this whole long-distance relationship was only going to make that reality even further down the line. But more than anything else, she believed that everything would work out as it should, so she wouldn't meddle, unless absolutely necessary.

She watched the two of them during the rest of breakfast, not saying much, which was highly unusual for her. Charles picked up the slack and talked with them about their plans after they arrived back home. The New Year was quickly approaching and Darren had to work on lesson plans while Kensi settled into her new position.

"We'll clean up," Darren offered. That was the least that he could do to repay the kindness they'd shown him during his visit.

"I won't say no to that!" Marie blurted, handing her plate and empty coffee mug to Darren. "We'll be waiting for y'all in the family room."

Darren filled the sink with dishwater while Kensi cleared the table. She hugged her father, thanking him for taking her side, and joined Darren at the sink. She was the designated dish rinser and he was the washer. Her phone began vibrating incessantly in her back pocket, so she stopped to read the messages.

Adam: *I'm glad to hear that you're coming back today. You were always more suited for this job than I was. I hope we can pick up where we left off before the whole promotion craziness.*

Kensi scoffed at the text, eliciting concern from Darren. She brushed it off as just a message about work without giving any explanation. She'd pretty much forgotten about Adam over the last month and had hoped that he'd done the same. She had no interest in being in the center of a love triangle just when it seemed everything was starting to fall into place in her life. The great guy. The dream job. Adam just didn't fit anymore. She hoped that wasn't the reason she finally got the job—so that he could get her back.

Chapter 29

Kensi and Darren exchanged hugs with Charles and Marie on the front patio before traveling to the airport. Marie adjusted Kensi's coat as she gave her advice one final time.

"All right, Ken Ken, you call me the minute you land in New York. I'm proud of you, but just remember that there is more to life than work. You need love too." Marie's attempt to speak softly in Kensi's ear was lost. Even when she thought she was whispering, she was far from it.

"I hear you, Mom. I love you. I love you too, Dad. Take care of yourselves."

"Young man, you're invited to spend next Christmas with us."

"Yes ma'am."

"I mean that! You don't need an invitation from Kensi."

"Got it," Darren said, chuckling at Marie's comment. He hoped that by this time next year, accompanying Kensi to her parents for Christmas wouldn't even be an issue. It would be a given. "Thanks for your hospitality. Everything was nice. I enjoyed myself."

Darren hugged Marie once more and shook Charles' hand. "Thank you for everything, sir."

"You're welcome. Just look after Kensi."

"You have my word."

Darren took Kensi's hand as they shuffled to the car to get out of the wind. He hoped he wouldn't be sick after experiencing summer, fall, spring and winter over the last few days. After helping Kensi inside, he waved to the Jacobsons once more and hopped inside the car. The engine and heat had already been running, so the car was nice and toasty.

"This is it, huh?" Darren said.

"Yeah. Back to the real world."

"This isn't real?"

"Yes, but things are about to be quite different now, don't you think?"

"We've gone down this road. It's nothing we can't handle. Right?"

"Right," Kensi agreed, trying to reassure herself. Talking about it was one thing, but experiencing it was completely different.

Darren honked the horn as he pulled out of the driveway. They waved good-bye to Kensi's parents, who were glued to the marble stone that covered the patio. Never mind that it was cold and windy, they still stood there to see the two of them off.

"I hope that child can get over the New York fantasy and give me my grandbabies," Marie commented.

Charles chuckled without responding to her comment. "Let's get inside and have some of your famous hot chocolate."

Because they had extra time on the way to the airport, they took the scenic route so that Kensi could show him a few places around town that he didn't get to see while he was there: hangouts, the old roller-skating rink, the town's favorite ice cream shop, her old high school, and even the place under the live oak tree in the city park where she had her first kiss. That was one memory he didn't care to hear about, but she shared it anyway.

The airport was not as busy as they thought it would be, considering it was only a couple of days after Christmas. For that, they were grateful. The check-in process went smoothly and allowed them a couple of hours to hang around before needing to board their flights.

They walked hand in hand through the airport, not really saying much of anything, just enjoying their time together. Kensi's mind reeled with thoughts of what would come next. Though she'd wanted the promotion, she wasn't sure what would be expected of her. Would she be able to get away to Pepperton once a month or every other month?

The last long-distance relationship she had was more than ten years ago, right out of college. That didn't work out for her, but she was much more mature and wiser now. Pepperton was a small town and she'd met many of the women there. Darren didn't seem to have an interest in them, so she had no reason to be jealous like she was before. Besides, the townspeople were nosey enough to get in his business and keep other women away.

The smell of freshly grilled hamburgers and the sound of Michael Jackson's *Beat It* enticed them to stop at Dave's Bar & Grill. They were still pretty full from the large breakfast Marie made for them, so they decided to share an appetizer. They ordered mini burgers, along with chips and dip, after settling into the small red leather booth.

"Since I have the most flexibility that we know of, I'll come out to see you in a couple of weeks," Darren said. "MLK holiday weekend work for you?"

"I don't see any reason why not."

Darren pulled out his phone to search flights and book his ticket. It was time to work their plan of making an extra effort. Though the video chatting would suffice on some days, he still needed to see her and spend time with her for their relationship to bloom the way he needed it to.

"Done. I sent a confirmation e-mail to you as well so that you can pick me up from the airport."

"Got it."

"I'm looking forward to a night or two on the town to see why you love this city so much. I can't imagine any city being better than P-town."

They burst into laughter at the thought. Pepperton had nothing on New York. Although Darren was settled there and thought it to be a much better place to raise a family, he was willing to agree that New York had far more going on than Pepperton.

Checking the time, they only had about forty-five minutes left before their flights were set to depart. Kensi had been in the airport enough times to know that the departure gates often changed and she didn't want to miss her flight. She already had a long evening ahead of her, considering she had a short layover.

Darren's steps became more hesitant when they made it to the area of the airport where they had to part ways. Their departure gates were on two different ends of the airport. "This is it."

"Don't be so sad. I'll try to have plenty of fun stuff planned when you come up in a few weeks."

"I know, but I've gotten so used to you being around, stalking me everywhere from the school, grocery store and even at *Pepperton Quad*. I just couldn't get rid of you, and now I don't want to."

"Ha ha ha. Very funny. I think I hear them making the announcement for the boarding of my flight. Don't try to hold me hostage so that I miss my flight and force me back to Pepperton."

"If I thought there was even the slightest chance of that happening, I would have been stalling from the moment you bumped into me this morning."

Kensi chuckled and moved to press her lips softly against his with one hand wrapped behind his head. "Be good. I'll talk to you tonight. Have a safe flight."

Slowly stepping away and sliding her fingers out of his, she turned to walk to her departure gate. Darren stood at the departure monitors and watched until she made it to her gate before turning to board his own flight. Being away from her for weeks and potentially months at a time was going to prove to be a testing of their faith. He'd never been in a long-distance relationship before, and even though he was sure they could make it work, it was going to be much harder than he thought.

Chapter 30

Adam hadn't spoken with Kensi since their fight on Thanksgiving Day when he called hoping to patch things up with her. He'd shaved his beard that he grew out for No Shave November. He looked so raggedy, it was a shame that he hadn't shaved it sooner. Now was as good a time as any though, since he was planning to surprise Kensi at the airport. He'd hacked into his grandmother's e-mails to find out when Kensi would be arriving. Technically it wasn't hacking since she left her computer unlocked; the e-mail from Kensi just happened to grab his attention.

Since he was the one who convinced his grandmother to make the assistant editor-in-chief job a joint position, he hoped that it was enough to salvage the relationship that had been budding between the two of them before the whole promotion fiasco. It simply didn't mean as much to him as it did to her. If it were completely up to him, he probably would be doing something else anyway. He was only there to keep the business in the family, as his folks would have liked, since no one else would do it.

He ran his fingers through his short blond cut, grabbed his keys, wallet and coat, and jogged down the steps of his brownstone apartment in Manhattan to hail a taxi to LaGuardia International Airport. He didn't know what type of reaction his presence would rouse out of Kensi, but he hoped it would be a good one, or else he'd look like a fool for going the extra mile.

Adam had the taxi driver stop by a local drugstore so that he could buy flowers and chocolate, with a promise to keep the meter running. He returned to the taxi with a bouquet of roses and a bag of Ghirardelli chocolate, and continued his journey to meet Kensi in baggage claim. Tipping the taxi driver, he arrived about ten minutes before her flight was set to arrive.

His uncertainty and anxiety were evident by the balls of sweat rolling along the side of his face, although it was twenty degrees outside and the temperature in the airport wasn't much higher. He walked around baggage claim to find where she'd be picking up her luggage. He paced around the area for at least twenty minutes until he heard his name being called. And from what he could hear, excitement did not lace her voice.

"Adam?" Kensi questioned. Confusion clouded her mind and her voice.

Adam looked up, grinning with a goofy look on his face, and held out the bouquet of roses and candy.

"What are you doing here?" Kensi asked, folding her arms across her chest, not yet taking the gifts from his hands.

"I came to surprise you! I've missed you around here!" Adam answered, still holding out the roses and candy for her. He thought his presence would have been obvious and at least greeted warmly, but instead he was starting to feel rejection. What happened to her over the last couple of months?

"I think you've surprised me enough for one lifetime. Don't you think?"

Adam rolled his eyes heavenward. Here we go again. She finally had the job and he was still going to hear about it?

"Let's be fair. You know that I have no control over what she does. Besides, you have the job now. Aren't you happy?"

"I guess that makes it all better then, right? Just forget about how you lied to me? About how you let me stroll into her office thinking she was about to offer me the job when you *knew* that she'd given it to you? And I do mean given . . . not *earned*," Kensi emphasized.

The ringing of the bell jolted her to her senses, reminding her that she no longer had to argue with Adam over what he did and didn't do. That was over. *Delta Airlines Flight 684* was now flashing on the kiosk, alerting her that her flight's luggage was up next. She shook her head in contempt and walked around him and stood at the moving conveyor belt waiting for her luggage to appear.

"All right, let's start over," Adam suggested. After he'd gotten over the fact that she'd left him standing in the middle of the floor and practically dismissed him, he followed her to the spot where she was standing near the luggage belt with her arms still folded across her chest. "I got these for you, please take them," he said and handed the roses and chocolate to her.

Kensi reluctantly accepted them and thanked him, though her voice was hardly above a whisper and she didn't appear to be thankful for the thought, not one bit.

"I really want us to start over, Kensi. I know that things didn't work out the way you planned and that somehow interfered with our relationship, but I want us to be *us* again. You know…getting to know each other better, dating, hanging out, facetiming. Do you think we can move past this?" *I have,* he added silently. He knew her well enough to know that would be a bad choice of words, because obviously she was having a hard time getting over it.

Kensi thought about Darren and how happy she was at the progress they were making. Even if Darren weren't a factor, she didn't think she'd be able to start over with Adam. That wasn't necessarily all his fault either. If Samantha didn't meddle in her life, then things would probably be different. The more she thought about it, the more she knew she needed to have a conversation with her about that as well—sending her to Pepperton because she didn't want Adam seeing her romantically outside of work. Going to Pepperton was not all business and she didn't have a right to do that.

"I can get past it, but you and I can't start over. So much has changed since we last talked." She contemplated whether or not she should tell him about the real reason that she was sent to Pepperton. She reached to pull her luggage from the belt, but Adam moved a little quicker and grabbed it for her.

"I don't mind." He took the bag and led her to the area where taxi drivers were already waiting. "What's changed? Why can't we start over?" Adam pressed.

"You should talk to Samantha. She knows everything. I'm sure she has *all* the answers," Kensi replied. The taxi driver put her luggage in the trunk as Adam helped her inside. He stepped back onto the curb as the taxi pulled off and sought out the next one. He'd pictured this going a lot different. He didn't think she'd be throwing her arms around his neck, but he expected a much warmer welcome than what he received. He wasn't going to sweat it; once she saw that he was giving up everything for her, she'd definitely want to start over. And as far as Samantha was concerned, the only thing he needed her to do was back him up.

Chapter 31

Kensi strode down the narrow hallway that led to her empty cubicle. She'd walked that hallway a number of times, but today felt different. The gray walls adorned with inspirational pictures and messages now felt lifeless; at one point, seeing *Success begins with you* or *Life is choice-driven* excited her about the day ahead and gave her an edge of hope that what she wanted was within her grasp.

When she arrived at her desk, a copy of the paper's edition that printed her article about Pepperton was sitting in her chair. She immediately thought of Darren and how he might be helping his students that day. Before unpacking and setting up her laptop, she sat in her chair and read through the article, smiling at the pictures she'd taken of the festivities.

"Great article," Adam said, startling Kensi. "Looks like you even had a great time while taking on this assignment," he added, pointing at one of the photos of her and Darren. A twinge of jealousy swept through his heart seeing a picture of her with another man. She looked happy in the photo.

"Thank you. I was just on my way to see Samantha. Has she made it to the office yet?" Kensi asked, not wanting to go into details about her time in Pepperton with Adam. She was trying her best not to give him an inch. The last thing she wanted to do was make him believe that they were going to pick up where they left off. From now on, she was only there to do her job, not to fraternize with him.

"She's running a few minutes behind, but I don't mind helping you get started," Adam offered and silently added, *I'm the reason you got the promotion in the first place.*

"Thanks Adam, but I can wait for Samantha while I get set up around here," Kensi said with finality, hoping that Adam would get the hint and stop hanging around her cubicle like a lost puppy.

"Do what you need to do. I'll stop by later." Adam wasn't fond of the dryness in Kensi's tone. She was acting like they didn't have a history together, almost as if they were complete strangers. Although the last few months had been rough for them, there was no erasing the great times they had together, at least not for Adam. He tapped the desk and walked away, giving Kensi her space for the moment.

Kensi exhaled when he walked away. That was pretty awkward, especially after last night's scene in the airport. She hadn't planned to tell him about Darren because it was none of his business, but maybe she would. She wasn't sure if the news would make him keep his distance or push back and try harder to rekindle their relationship. Either way, she'd have to break the news to him if he kept trying to pick up where they left off.

Kensi checked the time and called Darren. His first period was a conference period, so now was the perfect time to chat.

"I was just thinking of you. How is your first official day back in New York going? Missing P-town yet?" Darren joked, though he wished it to be true.

"Not bad. I'm waiting on Samantha to get here so that we can have our meeting. And umm . . . I'm not really missing P-town, only one special person who should probably think about moving to New York."

Darren chuckled. "I miss you as well. The next couple of weeks can't get here fast enough. This is going to be more difficult than I thought. It's only been what, a day and a half? And I'm already about to go crazy knowing that I can't see you at the end of the day."

"Well you know what they say, right?"

"What is that?"

"Distance makes the heart grow fonder."

"I don't need distance to teach me that. My heart grows fonder by the minute," Darren countered, his voice deep and serious.

"Well that's good to know. Have a great day, Mr. Shaw." Kensi cut the conversation short when she heard Samantha's voice down the hallway. Darren always had a way of turning playful moments into serious heartfelt talks, but now wasn't the time or the place for any of that.

"You do the same. Make sure your phone is fully charged this evening. We already have distance in between us; I don't need your phone clunking out on me just as we're facetiming."

"Anything for you."

"Be careful Ms. Jacobson. *Anything* will have you on the first flight out to P-town—for good."

"I bet," Kensi said and chuckled. "Later."

"Later."

"Oh, great, you're here!" Samantha sang, sticking her head around Kensi's cubicle, her gray hair dangling alongside her cheeks. "I'm ready when you are."

Kensi's heart fluttered nervously as she put her phone back inside her purse and slid her purse into her desk drawer. The time had finally come for her to walk the path that she always thought was meant for her, yet she was a little apprehensive. Thoughts of the reason that Samantha sent her to Pepperton in the first place swirled through her mind. The nerve of her to think that she could attempt to orchestrate who she should or shouldn't be with burned Kensi's insides.

If nothing else, Kensi was always a professional, so she'd find the right moment to tell Samantha to stay out of her personal life, all the while being gracious that she was finally given the opportunity to take the next steps in her career.

She followed Samantha to her office, careful to avoid eye contact with Adam when she passed by his office, which was stationed next to his grandmother's. She could feel his eyes burning a hole into her skull, but she was determined to ignore him.

"Have a seat!" Samantha seemed a bit more excited than Kensi remembered. It hadn't been that long since Kensi went away, but Samantha seemed different. She wondered what had changed. "Your work in Pepperton was amazing! You received glowing reviews from the Quad about your work with the trainees and the temporary assignment you took on. Tell me about the town. Did you meet anyone interesting? Any fascinating people or places in Pepperton?" Samantha asked. She gave Kensi her undivided attention. Eye contact, hands clasped in front of her with her elbows resting on the desk. She seemed genuinely interested, but Kensi knew different.

"Sandra didn't tell you?" Kensi skeptically asked. She wasn't going to go through this charade with Samantha. For a moment, she had planned to, but if they were going to work together, Samantha had to know that there were boundaries and she had clearly crossed them.

Samantha's eyes widened in surprise as if she had no clue what Kensi was referring to.

"I'm not sure I follow."

Kensi stood to close the door and returned to her seat.

"We can be frank, can't we? I know exactly what you did and why you did it. Pepperton took some getting used to, but I managed. I actually think I'm a better person for it. And yes, I did meet someone, so you don't have to worry about there being anything between me and Adam. But let's be clear, I love working and learning from you, but if you ever cross that line again, I'm gone." Kensi exhaled slowly when she finished her spiel. She hadn't planned to say things like that, but she couldn't hold back when Samantha brought her into her office, pretending like she didn't know what was going on.

"Understood," Samantha simply said, raising her hands from the desk in surrender. She had good reasons for doing what she did, but Kensi would never understand. She'd always viewed Kensi like a granddaughter and wanted the best for her, and that wasn't this company or Adam. Kensi had the potential to do so much more, but she needed to see that herself.

Adam didn't catch everything that was said between Samantha and Kensi, but he did hear *nothing between him and Kensi.* He needed some answers, but respected his grandmother enough not to barge into her office while she was in a meeting, even if it was with the woman whose heart he was trying to win back.

Samantha and Kensi spent the rest of the morning going through the transition and Kensi's official duties henceforth. Now that Kensi had gotten the pent-up anger off her chest regarding Samantha meddling in her life, she was ready for the opportunities that lay ahead of her. But she couldn't shake the sense that it didn't feel like she thought it would and that something was missing.

Chapter 32

"Me and my wool pea coat were not prepared for this weather! Woman, why do you choose to torture yourself like this?" Darren asked. His teeth chattered while he tried to warm himself in Kensi's car. Her car had been parked in the airport parking garage for no more than thirty minutes, but it was still freezing inside as if it had been parked there all day.

"Perk up! The heated seats along with this heat will warm you up in about two minutes. It's not as bad as you're making it out to be."

Darren's expression turned doubtful.

"Okay, maybe it is that bad, but see, it's already warm. Thawed yet?"

"That's better."

"How was your flight?"

"Not bad. I spent most of it anticipating being with you again, like I've done since we've parted ways a few weeks ago."

"Well I won't disappoint. We'll get you settled this evening, have dinner, and then we'll be out on the town tomorrow!"

Though Kensi was getting acclimated to her new role in the office, the last couple of weeks had been a blur for her. Just as Darren had been looking forward to their time together, so was she. She'd like to think that the anticipation helped her to become more productive. She was now in charge of her own editorial section, which mainly focused on the arts. She appreciated having the freedom of creativity in regards to planning new articles and having more of a voice in the direction of the paper. She had planned articles for the next couple of weeks so that she could push work to the side and focus on spending time with Darren when he arrived.

She took him to the hotel so that he could check in for the weekend before heading to her apartment for a while. They talked during the ride to Kensi's apartment as if they hadn't spent every night video chatting.

"What are we doing tomorrow?" Darren asked. Kensi had said that she wouldn't tell him until he made it to New York.

"We're going to see *The Lion King* on Broadway!" she squealed. That was one of her favorite musicals and she hoped that Darren would enjoy it. She'd promised that she'd take him to see and do activities that he couldn't do in Pepperton.

"I loved that movie as a kid."

"I know. And I also know that you're going to love the production. It's nothing short of amazing!" Kensi had seen it a couple of times already.

"Well amaze me. I've always wanted to see it . . . thought of taking the drive to Houston to catch it, but never made time for it."

Kensi's chest puffed out, proud of the selection of their first New York outing. That pride quickly turned into laughter as she watched Darren grip the support handle above the window.

"Tell me that we can take the train during the rest of my time here. I would like to make it back to Pepperton," Darren commented, keeping his eyes on the road as Kensi wove in and out of traffic, slammed on her brakes, and accelerated at a much faster pace than anyone would have anticipated.

"We can, but I can get us there faster. You can calm down. We're not going to crash. I have to drive like this so we won't get run over."

If that wasn't the craziest thing he'd ever heard, he wasn't sure what was. Pepperton was slow, but in this moment, he appreciated the slowness. He tried to recall if he'd ever ridden in a car with her driving and if she drove like that all the time. *Couldn't have,* he thought, because he would have insisted that they take another method of transportation from the airport. Even though he had once lived in Houston, he couldn't recall traffic being this horrible. By the time they arrived at her apartment, there were at least three moments when he thought he would lose his life in that car.

"God has spared me. My purpose has surely not been accomplished," Darren said and exhaled slowly as they pulled up to Kensi's brownstone apartment building in the Upper West Side of NYC.

"You really should stop that. It was not that bad . . . ooh a close parking space!" Kensi said, excited about being able to park in front of the building; she usually wasn't so lucky.

"Tell that to someone who was not in this car with you . . . and still, this is the life you choose?"

"C'mon inside before your toes freeze up and you have to crawl up these stairs," she teased.

"You're kidding, but it's not like it can't happen." Although Darren's coat was insufficient and it was windy and freezing, he walked slowly behind Kensi up the stairs into the building so that he could take in his surroundings. Crazy parking arrangements, buildings close together, no yard space, and yet there was still an element of charm to the area.

"Nice building."

"Thanks. Oh, let me warn you," Kensi said, turning around and stopping at the entrance to the building. "My apartment is small. Not the small that you're used to either, but don't judge. I don't want to hear your 101 reasons why Pepperton is better than NYC. Deal?"

"You won't hear it tonight."

"I guess I can live with that," Kensi said and unlocked the door so that they could go inside.

The apartment building somehow reminded Darren of a hotel, except that the floors were wood and the hallway walls had a little more color. It definitely held a city feel.

"Ta da!" Kensi announced when she opened the door to her apartment on the fifth floor.

"Wow." Darren couldn't believe how small her apartment was, nice, but small. He promised he wouldn't mention it, so he smiled and complimented her on the miniscule decorations. She wanted her space to feel somewhat cozy when Darren visited; so last weekend she purchased throw pillows for the sofa and a photo canvas of trees in every season, which she hung on the wall above the sofa.

"Hang your coat there," she said, pointing to a coat rack tucked away into a corner of the tiny living space. Darren did as instructed and followed Kensi into the kitchen to make hot chocolate, swapping kisses while their drinks were brewing. Returning to the living room, Kensi sat next to him, leaving little to no space in between them and continued to welcome him with passionate kisses.

"Umm," Darren groaned. "I guess that answers the question of whether or not you miss me too."

"Good," Kensi said, pulling away to sip her hot chocolate.

"Ahh, this is just what I needed to thaw out. I can't live like this."

"No one is asking you to," Kensi said, amused at his reaction. "Besides, it's just a little snow and it isn't always like this."

"Hmm . . . you may not be asking, but it's on the table. I know we kid around about it, but what will we do when our relationship gets to the point where one of us has to move?" Darren asked.

"I'm not married to New York. In all seriousness, I could and would move under the right circumstances, just not so sure about moving to Pepperton," Kensi answered truthfully and shrugged her shoulders.

"Now we're getting somewhere. We don't have to live in Pepperton forever, if you lived there for a while and decided you really didn't like it, but can we agree that New York won't work?"

"I like New York, but I'd never want to raise kids here, so I can agree to that."

"Yes! Answered prayer."

"Really?"

"Yep." Confirming that Kensi would be willing to move if their relationship progressed the way he hoped sent a wave of excitement through his core. Grinning, he placed his empty mug on the coffee table and pulled her into his arms, kissing her passionately.

"It's probably a good idea if we get out of here. Grab your coat, we're *walking* around the corner for Chinese. I promise it'll be the best you've ever had in your entire life," Kensi said after breaking the kiss.

Though it was freezing, he agreed. He hated to go back out in that ridiculous weather, but if they stayed in, he would surely break his promise of keeping his hands off her. They were in for a long weekend. Hopefully she'd thoughtfully planned his trip as much as she said she did.

Chapter 33

Kensi and Darren spent most of their time outside of his hotel room and her apartment in an effort to keep their hands off each other and risk moving their relationship to the physical level too soon, and outside of marriage. They spent several hours inside the Chinese restaurant after finishing their dinner, talking until they were exhausted enough to go to sleep.

The next day wasn't any different. After breakfast, Kensi kept her promise by taking Darren out on the town, and by foot or subway, since Darren was so afraid of her driving. That was probably the best method for them anyway since they made so many stops along the way.

"Is this for real?" Darren asked when they finished their tour of Chinatown.

"What?"

He missed the significance of touring Chinatown because he was caught up on the offers to purchase knockoff handbags, sunglasses, and accessories.

"How should I put this? Are the markets like this all the time? With people on the street trying to lure me into an unmarked building to sell me knockoff designer stuff?"

"Don't lose focus Darren. There are so many other significant cultural things to see, but I can catch a hint. Let's keep going so that you can see something a little different before our scheduled tour."

"It doesn't matter really. I'll go wherever you want to take me. Remember that this is your city. I think you're supposed to be impressing me."

They walked hand in hand, touring the streets of Manhattan. It was much like Darren had seen on TV: tall buildings, lit-up marquees, terrible traffic and congestion on the sidewalks. He was becoming annoyed by someone brushing up against his shoulders every so often to pass them on the sidewalk.

Taking a break at one of Kensi's favorite restaurants, Darren took the opportunity to people watch. Everyone seemed to be in a hurry, like there was no tomorrow. He couldn't understand why anyone would choose to live in such a congested place. Sure, there were nice things to do and places to visit, but it wasn't as if anyone could be doing those things all the time—enough to need to live there.

"How often do you get caught up in all the hustle and bustle?"

"Not much. I've spent so much time working and traveling over the past few years that I don't think I've gotten the chance to enjoy it enough. There's something euphoric about being in NYC, right?"

"Can't say I agree with you. You've yet to impress me."

Kensi laughed, probably a little harder than she should have. Darren didn't quite understand why that was so funny to her, but the laughter was contagious and he joined in for a few seconds as well.

"Well the day isn't over. We're taking the NYC gospel walking tour after this. I think you'll be impressed."

After brunch and coffee, they bundled up in their coats once more and headed toward the intersection of Wall Street and Broadway in front of Trinity Church, the starting point of the NYC gospel walking tour. The two-hour walking tour was much more fascinating than highlighted on TV. Along the tour, they learned the history of American gospel music and how it emerged, as well as observed beautiful homes and churches in Brooklyn Heights.

They also viewed the church that launched gospel music and ended the tour at a church where they heard some of the best gospel music in the world.

"Thoughts?" Kensi asked as they made their way back toward the train station.

"It was overwhelming, but fascinating. Now you're doing your job, Ms. Jacobson," he complimented and kissed her cheek. If there was any doubt about the temperature before now, the iciness of her cheek against his lips cleared it up. It was freezing and he couldn't wait to get inside and warm up, even if it was just for a moment since they would only be inside long enough to change before going back out to see the *Lion King* on Broadway.

∞

Chills covered their bodies as the opening chant to "The Circle of Life" rang through the theater, signaling the start of *The Lion King* on Broadway. Kensi had seen the show twice, but she sat and watched as if it were her first time. She'd watched the movie at least a hundred times and was amazed at how perfectly the actors brought the movie to life onstage.

Darren was captivated at the precision of the cast and their beautiful voices. From one act to the next, the flow, the face paint, the puppetry, the costumes, and the performance reminded him of the movie. He hardly moved an inch during the entire show and even sang along a time or two. Though he'd heard about the live performance, it was nothing short of spectacular, and worth every dime to see it for himself. He was far from the type of person who enjoyed musicals, but if they were even half as good as *The Lion King 360,* sign him up.

"So, what did you think?"

"I don't think I have many words to describe it. That was simply amazing!" Darren answered. When the curtains closed, they didn't move to exit the theater as everyone else did. "I'm a fan of the movie, but I think this was even better. Just wow!"

"I take it that means I've done my job and you're impressed."

"Impressed by the musical, yes. With the city, eh, it's all right. You being here is what makes all the difference."

Despite the dropping temperatures, Kensi had dressed up in a knee length, cowl-neck black dress. It wasn't often that she got the chance to dress up, and going to see *The Lion King* with the man she cared about was just as good an excuse as any to get all dolled up, even if she might have to pay for it later with a case of the sniffles. As they stood to leave, Darren helped her into her purple wool trench coat, wrapping her scarf around her neck before buttoning up his own jacket.

Hand in hand, they shuffled into the aisle and made their way out of the theater onto the sidewalk. Although people always seemed to be in a hurry, this time they had a reason: snow was falling like nobody's business, and if it kept up at the rate it was going, they would be stuck inside for the next day or so.

Chapter 34

Adam talked himself into reaching out to Kensi one final time. Instead of hailing a taxi, he opted to walk the fifteen blocks even though it had begun to snow. He'd changed his mind several times along his walk and almost turned around, but he couldn't let it go without pleading his case once more. The snow was covering the ground quickly and he was starting to see his footprints. He took that as another sign that he should turn around and go home, but something within him just wouldn't let him. He reasoned that he should probably check on her and make sure she had everything she needed since she would probably be snowed in by morning. He could have called, but she probably wouldn't even listen to anything he had to say. He held out hope that seeing him and how much he cared would stir something within her that would change her mind about them.

He had an eerie feeling that he just couldn't seem to shake when he arrived at the steps of her apartment. Was she all right? Did she need him? Did she miss him as much as he missed her?

He took a deep breath and reached for the buzzer to ring her apartment, but someone else opened the door to leave the apartments and allowed him to slip in. Showing up at someone's apartment who didn't want to see you could be creepy and considered stalking, but he didn't think Kensi would freak out.

Everything within him screamed that she wasn't ready to hear him out yet, but he chalked it up to fear, as he climbed the stairs instead of taking the elevator, to rehearse what he would say to her. He'd replayed the scene over and over in his mind during the walk over. It could only go two ways: either she let him in and they talked or she screamed at him and slammed the door in his face. Hopefully she'd show him a little compassion and at least offer him something warm to drink since he'd walked fifteen blocks in the snow to see her. That had to count for something.

Adam hesitated to knock when he heard the sound of laughter through the door. Was she watching TV? He leaned in against the green wooden door like the creepy stalker he convinced himself that he hadn't turned into, and listened for other voices. He was pretty sure he heard the voice of another man. Although the sound was faint, it was evident that Kensi wasn't alone. He considered going home, but he wasn't sure who was inside with Kensi. For all he knew, it could be her cousin or just another friend. He'd come too far to walk away now, so he tapped rhythmically on the door as he'd always done to alert her that it was him.

A range of emotions stirred within Kensi when she heard the knock on the door: disbelief, anger, frustration, and a little panic. Why would Adam show up to her place unannounced? Though she'd mentioned Adam to Darren once, she didn't want him to think that she'd started seeing Adam again when she returned to New York. Long-distance relationships are hard enough as it is; she didn't need Adam throwing in an element of distrust.

"Excuse me, let me get that," Kensi said, interrupting the conversation that she and Darren were having about his visit to New York.

She tiptoed and peered through the peephole as if she didn't know who was on the other side of the door. She took a deep breath and opened it, trying to appear unbothered by his spontaneous visit.

"How can I help you?" she asked when she opened the door. She stood in the doorway with her arms folded across her chest, as to not give him any indication that she would be inviting him in.

"I just want us to talk about what happened. It is not over between us, Kensi, and you know that. Why are you making a mountain out of a molehill?" he said, exasperated.

"I don't want to go through this with you again, Adam. There is nothing for us to talk about, and now really isn't a good time. We are expecting a blizzard. You should get home and bundle up," she said squarely.

"Dammit Kensi! You're not the first person to get overlooked for a promotion! Is that all you care about?" Adam's voice raised a few octaves, causing Darren to appear at Kensi's side immediately.

"I think you should leave. That is what you asked of him, right Kens?" Darren confirmed, wedging himself in between Adam and Kensi. His eyes never left Adam's. They were about the same height, but Darren had a muscular build as opposed to Adam. His stature alone could be threatening. He didn't consider himself a fighter, but he would not allow anyone to disrespect a woman in his presence, and certainly not Kensi—the woman he was falling hard for.

"Now it makes perfect sense. Kensi, you would have saved me a lot of embarrassment if you'd told me that there was someone else. Hell, I'm not even sure I would have fought for you to get that position if I knew this was happening," Adam said pointing to the two of them.

"Hold on. Are you trying to say that you're the reason Samantha gave me the promotion?"

"Exactly! I knew you deserved it so I went to bat with my grandmother on your behalf. For you Kensi!"

"No, you did it for your own selfish reasons. Let it go Adam. It's over." It bothered Kensi that Samantha didn't promote her based on her own merit, but because Adam had to lobby for her, if what he said was true.

"Maybe you should have stayed in Texas and saved us all the trouble" Adam said. He wanted her to hurt as badly as he did, no matter if she was good enough for the job. If they weren't going to be together again, he didn't want to work with her or see her face around the office every day.

Darren could feel Kensi advance against his frame, but he held her behind him. Kensi was just starting to move past all the promotion issues and Adam opened up the can of worms again.

"Good night Mister. I'm sorry, what is your name again?"

"Not important," Adam answered and walked away. A lump formed in his throat as he thought about the series of events over the last several months. Was he to blame for not standing up to his grandmother in the first place? Was Samantha the one to blame? Was it Kensi? The only thing he was certain of was that he wanted Kensi to hurt like he was hurting. Darren closed the door and reclaimed his seat and mug of hot chocolate on Kensi's couch.

He picked up their conversation where they left off, but Kensi was not on the same page.

"Hold on. So you don't want to talk about what just happened here? We can't just ignore it."

"I'm ready when you are."

"You do know that nothing is going on between me and Adam and hasn't been since I went to Pepperton, right?" Kensi asked. She'd finally moved from the spot on the floor where her feet seemed to have been glued, and reclaimed her seat next to Darren.

"I know that, but it doesn't seem like he does. Is he going to be a problem for you or for us?"

"I've honestly never seen him this way, so I don't know what to expect from him," Kensi said, shrugging her shoulders before taking a sip of hot chocolate. Adam's behavior did have Kensi a little worried, but she didn't want to mention that to Darren. Adam's eyes went dark the moment Darren moved to her side, and she didn't know what that meant. Work was probably going to prove to be difficult, but if nothing else, she was a professional and would keep Adam in his place.

"Promise to keep your distance from him. He might have a little craziness in him."

"That should be easy since you're the only man I want to be close to."

"Prove it right now."

Without hesitation, Kensi took his hot cocoa and gently placed it on the coffee table along with her own, curled onto his lap, wrapped her arms around his neck and kissed him passionately. Darren moaned against her lips as he returned the kiss. It was becoming harder and harder to keep his hands off her, but he still found the will to break the kiss.

"If you want me to keep my promise, you're gonna have to let me go back to my hotel right now or we're gonna be in big trouble, Ms. Jacobson."

Chapter 35

Darren looked forward to Sundays more than he did any other day of the week, because it was the time when he got his refreshing and his encouragement for the week. The snow that started falling last night was gone by morning, and for that he was thankful. He was looking forward to going to Living Word, the nondenominational church that Kensi attended when she was in town; he'd only gone to Baptist churches before now. After only being in New York a couple of days, he was taking the train like a pro to get from his hotel to Kensi's apartment. He arrived at her apartment early so that they could make it to service on time, but Kensi still wasn't ready.

They were a few minutes late, and when they arrived, the choir was in the middle of singing "Awesome" by William

235

Murphy. The entire congregation was on their feet, clapping, singing, and dancing along to the worship tune. When Kensi and Darren were shown to two empty chairs, they shrugged out of their coats and joined in worship.

Pastor Jeffries took the pulpit with the same amount of energy, continuing to sing and rock to the music, which was now playing a little softer. His prayer before starting the message sounded more like singing, which was met with Hallelujahs and resounding Yeses from the congregation.

He settled down and began to preach a message of hope from Luke 1:45, with a sermon title, "Blessed is the one who believes." He gave three major points during his message: 1. Learn God's promises. 2. Believe God's promises. 3. Expect God's promises to be fulfilled in your life when you live according to God's Word. After about forty minutes of preaching, Pastor Jeffries concluded his sermon with encouraging the parishioners to make their relationships with God a priority in their life.

"Church, God loves us. We know this because He gave His only Son for our sins. If God can give His Son, surely we can give Him us. Consider what your relationship with God is worth to you and commit your soul to Him today," Pastor Jeffries said and began opening up the doors of the church for prayer before offering and the benediction.

Kensi and Darren walked half a mile to Jimmy's Soulfood Kitchen after service. Bundled in hats, gloves, scarves and coats to brace themselves against the wind and chilly temperatures, they walked as quickly as possible, without much conversation, until they arrived at their destination.

Thankfully they were seated as soon as they arrived, ordering cups of coffee when the waitress approached their table.

"So, did you enjoy the service?" Kensi asked. She didn't move to take off her outerwear until the coffee arrived and she took a few sips.

"I got what I needed: Worship and a Word. Pastor Jeffries did a great job dissecting the Word. I can appreciate that. Praise and worship was energetic too. I can understand why you enjoy going to Living Word."

"Never left feeling any other way. I love it there."

"Got my soul fed, now I need to feed my stomach. I'm starving. Tell me what's good here." Darren put down the coffee mug and picked up the menu.

"We'll have to find out together." Kensi was eating there for the first time as well.

They both ordered the baked chicken, gravy covered rice, and vegetables. The next several hours they spent together convinced Darren more and more that their relationship could bloom into something greater.

∞

Six inches of snow on the ground would have been perfect if it was Christmas morning, but it wasn't and Darren had a flight to catch in a few hours. Closing the window shade, he was halfway disappointed when he saw that the city hadn't stopped for the six inches of snow that seemed to be melting, so he checked out of his hotel early that morning to spend his last few hours with Kensi before leaving town. A snowstorm would have been the perfect reason for him to extend his stay, but considering the fact that he was struggling to keep his hands off her, it was best that he left on time.

"Looks like the snow isn't sticking around after all," Darren said to Kensi when she passed through the living room on her way to the kitchen.

"I see that. I was looking forward to you being forced to experience New York City another day or two."

A hearty laugh erupted from Darren when he considered Kensi's comment. *Forced* was not the word he would use, more like convenience. It would be the excuse he would need to call in to work and request a substitute for the next couple of days. He joined her in the kitchen and hugged her from behind, planting a kiss on her cheek.

"Force? It would be my pleasure to spend any number of days with you, Ms. Jacobson."

Kensi poured two cups of coffee and turned around to hand one to Darren.

"One sugar, no cream, right?" she confirmed.

"Yes, thank you. So what are we having for breakfast?"

"Eggo waffles and scrambled eggs," she answered.

"No Oatmeal? No grits? No bacon or sausage?"

"It's either that or we brace the cold weather that you despise so much and go out for breakfast."

"I like waffles anyway. I was just wondering if you were going to throw in a sausage or something," Darren answered, quickly changing his tune at the thought of being in cold weather.

"Umm hmm. That's what I thought. I don't want my toes freezing off just because you're too good for my frozen waffles," Kensi teased.

"But this is your kind of weather."

"Yeah, but I don't have to be out in it just because I like it," she said over her shoulder as she grabbed the box of frozen waffles out of the freezer and the crate of eggs out of the refrigerator.

Darren offered to help with breakfast. He'd found a package of dinner sausage links in the fridge and checked the expiration date. Many of the items in her refrigerator looked like they hadn't been touched in quite some time. Though she purchased a few items for his visit, anyone looking inside her fridge would think differently.

"They're good. I threw out the expired stuff, well most of it anyway."

"Yeah, like this orange juice that expired two months ago?" he countered, holding up the carton with a November expiration date.

"Just cook the sausage smart alley . . . I said *most*. Besides, you have coffee or water, so it's not like you'll need anything else with your breakfast."

"Oh, but I do!"

In one motion, he tossed the sausage on the counter, pulled Kensi in his arms, and covered her lips with his. He'd convinced himself that he could kiss her without taking things too far; he knew how to stop before things got out of hand. But time after time, he was proved wrong as they got closer and closer to the line. This time, his hands were caressing the back of her neck, while her hands were caressing his back. She was lifting his shirt over his head when her cell phone rang with the distinctive ringtone that she'd assigned to her mother. Her mother always seemed to have bad timing when she called, but today it was probably a good time, since the will power they both thought they had was starting to dwindle.

"I'll just get started on breakfast," Darren said, pulling his shirt back over his hand as Kensi went to answer her cell phone. He shook his head as if to erase the thoughts that were swirling around in his mind. He hadn't been that close to another woman since Jessica, and he was starting to feel slightly guilty about really moving on, and for the fact that he allowed things to go so far with Kensi when he promised her that his intentions were to get to know her and not what was in her pants. He had to do better.

"Hey Mom, what's up?"

Though Kensi didn't have the phone on speaker, Darren could clearly hear every word that came out of Marie's mouth.

"Did Darren make it up there this weekend?"

"Yes ma'am, he's here. How are you guys doing?"

"Good . . . I'm just checking to see if I'm any closer to getting those grandbabies," Marie said, ignoring Kensi's question about their well-being. "What are y'all doing? How long is he there?" Marie continued.

"Would you like to talk with him, since it's obvious you're not really calling to talk to me?" Kensi asked while walking over to hand the phone to Darren, who had begun scrambling eggs and frying sausage.

"Good morning Mrs. Jacobson, how are you?"

"Even better now that I know that you two are trying to work things out, even though you live in two different parts of the country! Have you all decided which one of you is going to move? You can't keep up this flying here and there for too long now!" Marie carried on with her opinion about the status of their relationship.

"No ma'am. We're taking things slow," he said, not really believing that statement himself.

"Ah!" Marie grunted, clasping her chest. "How much time do you think you have on this earth? Just don't be *too* slow, all right? I can't be too old running up behind grandchildren."

"All right, that's enough," Kensi said and took the phone away from Darren before he could respond. He wasn't sure how to respond to that anyway other than to laugh. He liked Marie and knew what she desired most, so he didn't expect anything less of her on that call.

"Thanks for checking in Momma, we're good."

"I know. Just wanted to get y'all riled up a bit and start thinking about the stuff that matters. Your daddy said 'good morning.'"

"I love you all," Kensi said and blew kisses into the mouthpiece. "Talk to you later." Darren called out his good-byes before she ended the call.

After Darren finished cooking the sausage and eggs, Kensi jumped in and dropped the waffles in the toaster. She contemplated apologizing for her mother's directness, but thought better of it. Darren had met her and knew what she was like. She was a little rambunctious, but one thing she wasn't was wrong in this situation. Although this was only their first visit after deciding to make it official, one thing for sure was that they weren't going to be able to go on like this.

As they sat across from each other enjoying breakfast and small talk, Darren thought more about the future of their relationship. Although things were going well, he was certain of one thing: he didn't want a *once-a-month* girlfriend. He wanted someone he could build a life with, and he wasn't sure how they were going to do that hundreds of miles apart, but he was still willing to give it a shot with the hope that the distance wouldn't be an issue for too long.

Chapter 36

Adam held true to the vow he'd made to himself—to give Kensi hell. She was going to regret not choosing him. He knew he should draw a line between personal and professional aspects of his life, but that was hard to do when the woman who broke his heart not only strolled past his office door every day, but her duties overlapped his from time to time and he had to work closely with her.

Week in and week out, though they shared the same level of seniority, he shot down her ideas, passed on additional assignments to her, or purposely provided untimely feedback so that she would have to work late. Sure, he was being petty and allowing his feelings to dictate his actions, but a tiny part of him rejoiced at her frustration. Though she tried hard not to show it, he knew her well enough to know that she was agitated. It was good that she was being the bigger person, because he had no plans to be.

The very thought of having to work with Adam made Kensi grind her teeth. She worked to keep her distance as much as she possibly could, but that proved difficult since it seemed that he was hell bent on going out of his way to cause her grief. She passed on the offer to work in an office, which was next to Adam's, with the excuse that she wanted to remain personable by keeping her cubicle.

It had been nearly a month since Darren's visit and their run-in with Adam at her apartment, so she was looking forward to visiting Darren in Pepperton at the end of the week. She didn't care what Adam threw at her this week—nothing was going to stop her from getting on that plane. She'd thought of talking with Samantha about Adam's behavior, but she'd just be playing right into his hand. Besides, she could handle herself. She hoped that Adam would grow up and move on with his life eventually, instead of focusing on what she had going on in hers.

"Knock, knock," Adam said, simultaneously tapping on her cubicle partition. Without waiting for her to acknowledge him, he said, "I need you to take over for me during a lunch meeting I have scheduled with the producer of the upcoming Broadway play, *Shaken.*" Samantha needs me to take over for her at another meeting, so we could really use your help today.

Rats! Kensi tried to hide her grimace. Adam knew how much she valued her lunch break, which she often referred to as *Me time.*

"My pleasure. Anything else?" she responded as kindly as she could muster. She never turned away from her laptop screen to look at him. Adam was just looking for attention and a reaction to his antics, but she refused to give him any.

"That's all for now, thank you," he said dryly. He was slightly upset that she didn't turn to look at him, but he let it go and pivoted on his heel to walk away.

"Oh yeah, I'll be stopping by the burger joint down the street on the way back into the office. Want me to pick up a burger or salad for you?"

"I'm good. Thanks."

He had a lot of nerve to think that he could play nice and dirty at the same time. What did he think was going to happen? That she would swoon over a sandwich and salad? If he did, then it was clear that he didn't know her at all. When his footsteps became faint, she pulled out her cell phone and texted Darren.

Kensi: Honey, I have to cancel our lunch video chat today. I have to sit in for Adam at a meeting.

Darren: Still pulling stunts, I see. Don't allow him to bring you to his level. Continue being the awesome woman and professional we all know you are! I miss you.

Kensi: You know he is. I'm trying but he is getting on my nerves.

Darren: I'll be sure to help relax them this weekend.

Kensi: Can't wait to see you tomorrow! I'll get back with you after my meeting.

Darren: Do what you do best. ♥

Kensi: ♥

She despised last-minute changes, and this meeting was one of them. She knew Adam purposely waited until the last minute to request her assistance with the producer. She quickly researched the producer and the upcoming musical so that she could have her own questions to ask. Anything that had her name on it would be done well, so despite her issues with Adam and vice versa, she would still put her best foot forward.

Kensi stood in the elevator bank, accompanied only by the soft jazz music that played through the intercom. She checked her hair and clothes in the mirrored panel as she waited for Marcella Bloomsdale to arrive on their floor. When Marcella arrived, Kensi escorted her through the office, where Kensi introduced her to Samantha before settling into the conference room. Kensi was grateful that their office receptionist had ordered refreshments. She'd been so hell bent on ignoring Adam and making sure that she made a good impression that she'd completely forgotten about other accommodations. She was grateful to walk into the room and see that coffee, water, a fruit tray and sandwich tray were already spread across the table. A bit much for two people, but she was grateful nonetheless.

Kensi and Marcella immediately hit it off. They spent the entire meeting discussing the production as if they were old friends, and Marcella treated her as such, offering Kensi VIP passes for the production. Opening weekend was set to be around the same time that Darren would be visiting her in March. After gathering the information that Adam requested, she thanked Marcella for her time and walked her back to the elevators.

As Marcella entered the elevator, Adam was getting off. He attempted to make small talk, but Kensi didn't entertain him. Instead, she gave him a quick summary of the meeting and indicated that she would have notes available for him within the next hour.

Although Kensi enjoyed her meeting and kept up her end of the bargain by giving Adam her notes, she was out of favors for the week. She took the rest of the day off to prepare for her trip back to Pepperton. There was no way she would allow herself to get stuck in the office before getting on that plane. She was more than ready to be in Darren's arms again, and she wasn't planning on letting anything get in her way.

Chapter 37

What a difference a few months can make! When Kensi boarded the plane for Pepperton the first time, it was not of her own volition. She felt betrayed and angry and was just ready to get it over with. This time, she met the trip with great anticipation and hoped that the time would move as slowly as possible so that she could spend many hours with Darren before heading back to New York.

Five and a half hours later, Kensi finally arrived in Pepperton. She couldn't get out of her seatbelt fast enough to get through the exit. She hurriedly walked to the front of the crop-duster, at times walking sideways to get past other passengers, grabbed her bags at the jetway and all but ran through the airport to meet Darren in the baggage claim area.

"Hey!" Darren said, scooping Kensi off her feet into his arms. For a moment, they were the only two in that airport as their lips pressed together. For the life of him, Darren had no idea how he could keep this up. It hadn't been but a few months, but it felt like forever to him. Something had to change. Soon.

As if they could manage time themselves, they slowly walked hand-in-hand to Darren's car. The warmer temperature did not go unnoticed as Kensi started to perspire. She was dressed in a ribbed sweater and boots, while everyone else appeared to be dressed in pastel-colored short-sleeved tops and pants. It was clear that spring was in the air, and New York hadn't received the message.

"I almost forgot that we're in two different worlds when it comes to weather," Kensi said and chuckled, tugging on the neck of her sweater to allow air to flow through.

"Based on how you're dressed, I'm guessing it's near zero in the city, huh?"

"Yeah."

"Even though you look like a foreigner, you're still beautiful. Who cares that you're dressed like a snowstorm is about to come through!"

"The whole town cares, I'm sure."

"None of what they think or say is going to stop me from loving you. You know that, but we will need to get you changed."

Kensi stopped mid-stride at what she thought was a profession of love. She knew how he felt about her, even though he'd never actually said so.

"What did you say?"

They were only a few steps away from his car, so Darren tugged on her hand to keep her moving until they were standing by the passenger door. The words had pretty much slipped out of his mouth. That wasn't the way he wanted to tell her. He would have liked for it to be a little more romantic than that, but you could only conceal the truth for so long.

"I said you need to get changed out of that sweater." He moved to put her bags in the trunk and returned to her side to open the car door.

"And?" Kensi couldn't move to get into the car until she was certain she heard what she thought she heard.

Darren inched closer, held Kensi by the waist, and stared into her eyes for a moment. She tried hard to mask her smirk. It was just like Darren to dramatize the moment.

"And I said there isn't anything that anyone can say or do to stop me from loving you. I love you Kensi Jacobson. I do. And it's *killing* me that you're so far away from me and I have to wait weeks at a time to see you. But for you, I'm willing to wait until we can somehow work this out so that we can be together every day," Darren answered, his voice gentle yet firm and confident.

251

"Always so thorough," she teased, fingering the collar of his shirt. Her smile widened as she couldn't hold back the joy she felt from hearing him profess his love for her.

"I love you too, Mr. Darren Shaw." Kensi locked her fingers around his neck and sealed her profession with a kiss before sliding into the passenger seat and securing her seat belt. At that moment, she wished there was something that would stop her heart from beating like it was going to pop out of her chest. All she could do was use the few seconds it would take for him to join her in the car and try to control her thoughts and her breathing.

Something about putting their professions of love on the table made Kensi want to pack her bags and move to Pepperton at once. She couldn't believe that she was actually starting to seriously consider it. But wasn't it too soon for that? There were rules against moving and shifting your life around for another person. You simply weren't supposed to do that without some sort of commitment. Was she even ready for that level of commitment with Darren? As much as she'd dreamed about being married, being ready for it was an entirely different thing. One thing was for sure, love was in the air and there was no turning back.

Chapter 38

Even though Kensi spent the night in Pepperton Inn, the fact that she was nearby didn't give him solace because he couldn't touch her. Though he'd fallen asleep in that worn, leather recliner chair more than a hundred times, he couldn't sleep comfortably for anything. His mind and spirit warred with each other all night long. He was reminded of his lack of sleep when Kensi appeared at his front door with a huge smile covering her face, clearly well rested.

"Good morning! What's the plan for today?" she sang, pecking his check and sauntering into the kitchen, dressed in a green V-neck T-shirt and blue jeans, with her hair pulled back in a ponytail.

Darren reached for Kensi's hand and pulled her into his arms. "Wait, come back here. It's been like ten hours since I last saw you and that's all I get?"

Kensi wrapped her arms around Darren's neck, squeezed gently, and kissed him more passionately than she did a few moments before. "Better?"

"That's more like it. I haven't seen you in months. You can't be acting like I see you all the time with that lil' sorry peck on the cheek you gave me when you walked in here."

Kensi acknowledged his comment with a giggle and proceeded to rummage through his kitchen cabinets for coffee mugs.

"In the top cabinet to the right of the refrigerator," he instructed. She didn't ask about the mugs or coffee, but he knew she loved her morning brew. He returned to his recliner and watched her, his chin resting on his fist, thinking about what it would be like to have her in his kitchen, well their kitchen, every morning. He smiled at the thought.

"Thanks. Speaking of acting like we see each other all the time, why haven't you made any coffee yet?"

"You're better at it than I am," Darren teased.

"Whatever. Want some?" she asked, taking a coffee mug from the shelf, moving around the kitchen like it was her own. She busied herself to muster up the courage to ask him about Jessica.

They'd talked about her before, but Kensi wondered if he was really ready to move on. It had been five years since Jessica died, and in her mind, that was enough time to grieve, but she wasn't in his situation, and she needed to hear it directly from him. She needed to make sure that she wouldn't have to compete with his past.

"After coffee, let's go out for breakfast. There's a place I'd like you to try."

"No problem. You're the captain today." She filled both mugs and joined him in the living room, handing one to him and taking a seat across from him on the sofa. She took a sip of her coffee to collect her thoughts before bringing up the subject of his deceased wife. Life had been all kinds of crazy for her lately, so this was one thing that she wanted to discuss, especially with the expression of love they'd shared. She didn't want to go all in only to find that he changed his mind and decided that he wasn't quite ready.

"What's on your mind?"

"Hmm?"

"I've noticed that you do this strange thing with your lips when you want to talk about something. What is it?"

"Am I that obvious?" she asked, wrapping the warm coffee mug between her fingers as if it were a security object.

"Yeah, you are. What is it?" Darren pressed. He'd seen that look before; it showed uncertainty. He hoped that she wasn't trying to find the words to take back her *I love you.* That would surely send him out of his mind, since the next thing on his agenda was engagement. His chest tightened as the moments of silence passed between them and he anticipated what would come next.

"Let's talk about Jessica."

"Wooo!" Darren exclaimed. An audibly loud breath escaped his lips as he placed his hands across his chest for a moment to calm his breathing. "You scared me for a minute there . . . okay, what do you want to know?"

"I want to be sure that your heart is ready for this, for us." Kensi couldn't believe she'd actually expressed that; she felt so vulnerable in that moment.

Up until that moment, Darren had still been reclining. He returned the recliner to an upright position, got up and joined Kensi on the sofa. Pulling out the ring that he'd bought for her would probably convince her, but now was not the time; he still planned to ask her parents for her hand in marriage. So instead, he tried his best to verbally explain that his heart was available only to her.

"Kens, Jessica was a beautiful woman, inside and out, but she is no longer here with me. God smiled down on me and gave me a second chance at love when He brought you into my life, and I have been thanking Him daily for that." He gently removed the coffee mug from her hands and set it on the table, encircling her hands in his before continuing. "It's me and you now, for what I hope to be a very long time. Jessica will have a place in my heart, but no one's place is as big as yours. I meant every word yesterday. I love you, Kensi, and I hope to get a chance to show you that every moment I get." He had to stop before he found himself proposing anyway.

"I love you, too."

Kensi's anxiety lifted after he shared his feelings. She didn't know what it was like to lose a spouse, and she wasn't going to pretend to know. Just as much as him, she was glad to be getting her shot at this kind of love and happiness.

∞

CeCe's Country Kitchen was packed as always during Saturday's breakfast hours. The smell of pancakes and bacon wafted through the parking lot as Darren and Kensi made their way to the entrance. He walked right past the line up to the hostess stand.

"We don't have to stand in line, honey," he said to Kensi when she took her place in line.

"Our party is here already," Darren said to the hostess when he saw Caleb and Raegan waving them over.

"Ahh!!" Kensi squealed, releasing Darren's hand to run over and squeeze Raegan. "It's so good to see you! What are you guys doing here?" Kensi exclaimed, releasing Raegan and walking over to hug Caleb, who was seated with the twins in his lap. She kissed the twins on the cheeks and walked over to Nicholas, who kissed her cheek and hugged her.

"We had to come see if Pepperton really existed!" Raegan joked. "Darren invited us."

"Are you trying to earn cool points with me, mister?" she asked before pressing her lips against his.

"Depends. Does this get me any?"

"Mmm. Maybe."

Darren and Kensi joined the family at the table after Kensi relieved Caleb of one of the twins. Kensi felt like she was surrounded by family, and this was what she needed after the craziness going on at work with Adam. Darren was definitely her kind of guy—anticipating and giving her what she needed before she could even ask. If this was what she had to look forward to, being all in was going to be easy.

Chapter 39

Kensi repeatedly lifted the baby in the air until a stream of milk erupted from his lips and down her T-shirt, puddling in the middle of her bra. Quickly, she handed the baby back to Raegan and walked toward the restroom to clean herself. Feeling the warm liquid roll down her chest was definitely not something she was used to.

"Kensi, is that you?" Kensi spun around at the sound of a familiar voice. It had to be Miss Sandra. There was no other country drawl like hers.

"Hey, how are you?" Kensi surprised herself by extending her arms for a hug, forgetting her shirt was soaked with milk. It was actually great to see Miss Sandra. Up until now, she hadn't realized that she missed working with her.

"Doing as good as a full fly on a hot summer day!" Miss Sandra answered, squeezing Kensi like she was an old friend. "Ooh," Miss Sandra jumped back when she felt the wetness.

Kensi giggled at her response. She had no idea what that meant, but expected nothing less from Miss Sandra.

"Oh sorry," Kensi apologized, tugging at the front of her shirt as if that would help. The damage had been done. "I take it that means you're doing well."

"Of course! We miss you around here! Are you back in town for good?"

"No, just visiting," Kensi answered. She turned her head toward Darren and smiled.

Waving at Darren, Miss Sandra's eyebrows shot up. "Good for the two of you! I won't get in your business, but," Miss Sandra held Kensi by the hands and whispered, "if and when you decide to come back, come see me. I'll have a spot waiting for you."

"Umm thanks," was all Kensi could say. She excused herself and continued on her journey to the restroom.

The moment Kensi was out of ear and eyeshot, Raegan urged Darren to show her the engagement ring. Caleb and Raegan gushed over the princess-cut diamond Darren bought for Kensi.

Darren had kept in contact with the couple since their first meeting, so they were aware that he wanted to marry her, but didn't have many more details. All Darren had said was that he was waiting on the right time.

"So how long are we talking about waiting here?" Raegan probed.

"I want to talk to her parents first. I'm a little old-fashioned."

"How long is it gonna take you to do that?"

"Do what?" Kensi asked, reappearing much faster than Raegan would have liked. She wasn't finished getting the scoop. Now that she'd seen the ring, she had many unanswered questions.

"Oh, nothing really. Just talking about doing some work around the house and Mr. Handyman over here added that he's going to paint his house by himself."

Both Caleb and Darren found it interesting that Raegan was able to come up with a lie that quickly, especially since home remodeling had nothing to do with their conversation. Caleb made a mental note to check her on that later. There was no telling how many times she'd done that to save her skin.

"Rrright," Darren slowly agreed.

"Oh, I didn't know that."

"I didn't want to bore you with the details, unless you don't mind picking up a paint gun?"

"Kensi is pretty handy. Don't underestimate her. Not that you two care, but I think that's the perfect opportunity for her to show you what she's got. My girl can fix door hinges, change out pipes under the sink, and use a drill."

"So why haven't you taught your friend here?" Caleb chimed in.

"I have you, honey, no need for me to learn any of that."

"So you only have me around to fix things for you?"

"Among other things," Raegan teased before puckering her lips to kiss him. "You know I love you more than anything."

"I do."

Kensi rolled her eyes and turned her attention to the menu. If they kept up the mushiness, another set of twins was surely on the way. Darren leaned in toward Kensi, placing his right arm across the back of the seat, and pointed out breakfast dishes that he had tried and thought she might like. After she decided on an egg, sausage and hashbrown scramble with a side of pancakes and placed her order, Raegan passed one of the twins to her. Although Kensi didn't ask to hold the baby again, she welcomed the cuddly infant back into her arms. Raegan was mostly trying to screen a reaction from Darren, and that is exactly what she got. Neither

Raegan nor Caleb missed the way Darren's eyes lit up watching Kensi coo at the baby girl.

Kensi looked perfect holding Raegan's baby, and that was one thing Darren was looking forward to sharing with her. He had to shake his head to push the thoughts aside, given it wasn't something that they'd discussed in detail, nor was it even time for any of that yet. He was constantly reminding himself to slow down and allow time to help them grow together.

When their food arrived, Kensi refused to hand the baby back to Raegan, claiming that she didn't get a chance to see them much and wanted to hold them as much as she could while she was in town.

"That's an easy fix. Just move to Texas," Raegan advised. "Houston, Pepperton, somewhere nearby. That way we could all get a chance to see you as often as we'd like." Raegan winked at Darren. His smile grew wide at Raegan's recommendation. For once, he didn't have to be the one to say it. Everything that she wanted and needed was in Texas. It wasn't like her career would suffer; she could easily work remotely or make her mark in Pepperton. But he would never suggest that she do that until he'd given her a commitment. Even then, he wanted moving to be something that she wanted and not something she felt like she *had* to do.

"It's not as easy as it sounds. My life is in the Big Apple."

"Start a new one," Raegan challenged her.

"I guess you have all the answers, huh? Mrs. I already have my house, husband, children and career. That's easy for you to say when everything is neatly wrapped and packaged."

"I didn't say it was easy. I'm just saying that—"

"Move to New York! All of you!" Kensi interrupted, hoping to prove her point.

"Can't. I think we're pretty settled here, right babe?" Raegan asked Caleb, who nodded in agreement.

"And I'm not settled? Wait, never mind, don't answer that question. . . . I'll just keep visiting for now. Maybe at least one of you," she paused and glared at Darren before continuing, "will decide to make a move."

"I have faith that you'll change your mind soon," Darren countered.

"Me too Darren! And Kens, life can change in an instant, girlfriend!" Raegan emphasized her final thoughts with the snap of her fingers.

Raegan almost hated the fact that she knew that Darren was going to propose, because she wanted so badly to tell Kensi. Surely Kensi knew that it had to be coming, but Raegan wished that she could be around to witness the proposal and Kensi's face to see if she would be singing the same tune about staying in New York after the proposal.

Chapter 40

Their weekend together ended way too quickly for Darren's taste, but he had hope that this whole back-and-forth business would be coming to an end soon. His plan was already set in motion. He could scratch off another item on his list: her parents agreed to his visit, unbeknownst to Kensi.

His plane was set to depart a couple of hours after Kensi's. He'd already packed his bags in the trunk of his car without Kensi knowing. He would sit in the airport with her until it was time for her to leave and then do his own check-in.

After church, Darren and Kensi went to Pepperton Seafood Shack for lunch.

"I have been secretly craving the food here. How did you know?"

"I didn't, but thanks for telling me. That means that Pepperton has been on your mind more than you'd like to admit."

"I didn't say that. Just saying the food is good."

"Ummm hmm," Darren agreed, inhaling deeply to relish in the smell of smoked meat. "Same table?"

Kensi nodded and Darren led the way. She waved and smiled at the familiar faces she passed on the way to their seat. It was weird how this place sort of felt like home to her. They were immediately greeted by their waiter, and without accepting the menu, Kensi placed the same order as she did on her first visit.

"I'll take the same thing."

"The entire crop-duster is going to smell like this place!"

"Yeah, one whiff of you and every passenger on that thing is gonna want to eat. Just please don't let them eat you. I don't know what I'd do if I couldn't see you again," Darren exaggerated.

"Speaking of," Kensi said after giggling at Darren's comment, "we need to plan your visit to New York! I have free tickets for the new Broadway production, *Shaken.* Interested?"

"What's it about? Wait, don't answer that. It honestly doesn't matter. My time there is all about being with you, no matter what we do."

Kensi blushed. "I can dig it."

Even with the after-church crowd, the chefs still managed to get their food to them a lot faster than the couple anticipated. They were interrupted at least three times by parents who recognized Kensi from the Christmas production. They all wanted to know about her well-being and if she was back in Pepperton for good. That was one thing she wasn't sure if she liked or not— either the Peppertonians were observant and she stuck out like an orange in a strawberry patch, or they were nosey and trying to determine what was going on in her relationship with Darren.

They still had about an hour on their hands after finishing their lunch before Kensi needed to be in the airport, so Darren suggested that they walk through Pepperton Central Park. They strode out of the restaurant and walked the short distance to the park. The temperature had to be about seventy-two degrees while the sun shined perfectly. A gentle breeze touched them every now and again. It was as if God Himself encouraged the interaction.

This was the kind of life that Darren wanted—peaceful and harmonious with Kensi. This could be something they did together every Sunday after church service, taking long peaceful walks in the park.

At first, they didn't talk much until Darren brought up the subject of children.

"How many children do you want to have, Kensi?" Darren asked casually.

Though the question caught her off guard, it was not something she was unprepared to answer. Children had been a subject she'd often thought about as she considered herself growing older.

"At least two but not more than four. You?"

"As many as you'll give me."

Kensi's steps slowed to a stop.

"Whoa! Way to make this personal!"

"It is personal, isn't it? I think there's a part of you that doubts how serious I am about you, about us," Darren said, as he caressed her chin with his free hand. He led Kensi to a nearby park bench positioned in the shade of a live oak tree. As they sat, he stretched one arm across the bench while Kensi made herself comfortable against his frame.

"I'm intentional," Darren continued. "I'm not just dating you for the fun of it. I see the woman that I'd like to spend forever getting to know." Darren felt the ring box press against his chest as he reached across to hold Kensi's hand. He wasn't sure why he continued to carry it around as if he were waiting for the right moment. That moment couldn't come until her parents agreed that they would give her away, though her mother seemed to be convinced already. Her father's approval was the one that would seal the deal.

"It's good to know that we aren't wasting one another's time," Kensi responded. She kissed him tenderly and stood, as they needed to begin walking back to his car so that she would make it to the airport in enough time to catch her flight.

"I love you, Kensi."

"And I love you, Mr. Shaw."

∞

Kensi checked in for her flight about an hour early. Considering the airport was so small, she still had a few minutes to hang around with Darren before going through the security gates. They spent the rest of the time booking his flight and making plans for his next visit to New York City.

After making his travel arrangements, Darren pulled a card from his suit jacket. "Happy Valentine's Day beautiful!"

When Kensi opened the card, The Temptations hit, My Girl, began to play and Darren sang along. He then pulled a small square box from his pocket and handed it to her. He'd already purchased a camera and ice skate charm to adorn the bracelet.

"These are to remind you of me. As we create memories together, I'll continue to add to it."

Kensi threw her arms around his neck and thanked him. "Valentine's Day was last week and I didn't bring anything for you. I have to make it up to you when you come to visit."

"Oh but you did – you! That's all I want. And I trust that if there was ever any making up you needed to do, the next time I visit, we'll get it squared away."

With her arms still wrapped around his neck, she leaned forward and kissed him. If the time they'd already shared hadn't been enough, that moment alone made her want to stay in Pepperton with him.

Before long, she could hear the call for her flight over the PA system. She gave Darren one last lingering hug and kiss and made a beeline for the security gates. Her departure gate was just on the other side. Since there wasn't a long line, she could be at her gate in about ten minutes.

"Call me the moment you land!" he called out to her from the other side of the security gate.

Darren returned to his car to retrieve his bags from the trunk. He only planned to be away for a couple of days. Though he could have waited until the following weekend to visit her parents, he chose not to; now seemed to be as good a time as any. He wanted to get her parents' approval as soon as possible because as far as he was concerned, his next trip to New York was certain to be the last one he would take and return to Pepperton alone.

Chapter 41

"Show me Your favor, Lord," Darren prayed as he navigated the rental Jeep to the Jacobson residence. When he was there with Kensi for the Christmas holidays, he felt positive vibes from her parents, so he wasn't sure why he was nervous now. *What if they didn't give their blessing?* Darren never really considered the possibility that they would say *no*. In fact, he was certain this was a mere formality and a sign of showing her parents respect and an opportunity to lay out his plans for his and Kensi's future.

Darren stepped out of the car, adjusted his clothes, and grabbed the small brushed metal gift bag. He didn't want to go overboard and appear as if he was trying too hard, but he did want to bring a small token to show that he thought about them. Darren had printed a photo that Shana captured of the couple along with

Kensi's parents and placed it inside a curved glass frame with the word *family* embossed along the sides in cursive writing.

Confident, Darren marched to the front door with the gift in his left hand. As he lifted the right hand to ring the doorbell, the door flung open with a squeal from Marie.

"Darren!" she all but yelled. She lifted her hands toward heaven and said, "Thank You for answering my prayers, Lord! Come in! Charles!"

"It's good to see you too! How are you, Mrs. Jacobson?" he asked after pulling out of her embrace.

"Oh, none of that nonsense. Just call me Marie, or even Mom," she hinted and winked.

"This is for you guys. Just a small token to let you know I was thinking about you."

Marie peeked inside the bag, gushed over the picture and ushered Darren into the kitchen where Charles was sitting, getting ready for a late dinner.

"Sir." Darren extended his hand to Charles, who gripped firmly and shook.

"Good to see you, son," Charles said. "Please, sit and have dinner with us."

Darren hadn't had much to eat besides airport snacks since the lunch he'd had with Kensi earlier that afternoon, so he eagerly accepted the invitation to dine. In fact, he was hoping that there would be something good to eat when he came. The last thing he wanted to do was eat hotel or fast food after such a long day.

With all of the food Marie was piling on his plate, one would have easily assumed that it was the holiday season again. Mustard greens, cornbread, hen, macaroni and cheese, cornbread dressing, green beans, and sweet potatoes all landed on his plate, Chocolate cake and apple pie were on the menu for dessert.

"Do you always cook like this?"

"Yes, she does. No other reason I'd be walking around looking like this," Charles answered and patted his big belly as evidence of Marie's cooking as though for a large family when it was usually only the two of them.

"Don't put that on me, Charles! It's not like I'm forcing you to eat. Besides, I don't cook on Mondays. We eat leftovers. I knew you were coming to visit, so I wanted to make sure that you had a good meal when you got here," Marie explained herself. "It's not like you're getting a good home-cooked meal every day. You could use a little nourishment." Marie peered over her specs and eyed Darren's lean frame, but made no more mention of it. He considered himself muscular and fit. His biceps were well trained and he didn't have a hint of body fat.

"I can appreciate that."

After lumping enough food on Darren's plate for two people, Marie made her own plate and joined the men at the table. Charles murmured a quick prayer before shoving a forkful of mustard greens into his mouth. Mealtime conversation was mostly filled with what Darren had been up to since his last visit. Marie had spoken to him on the phone while he was visiting Kensi or vice versa, but nothing more than a couple of minutes. When dinner was over, Marie brewed a pot of coffee and ushered the men into the living room so they could get down to the reason for Darren's visit. If it were up to her, they would have gotten straight to business before Darren could get through the door, but before Darren arrived, Charles urged Marie not to rush things. She was one step closer to getting the grandbabies she wanted, so it took everything within her to harness her self-control.

She glided into the living room with three coffee mugs on a serving tray. After making sure that both men had their drinks, she grabbed hers and set the tray on the coffee table before curling up next to Charles on the sofa.

"Thank you," said Darren. He took a sip of his coffee and placed the mug on the coffee table. Clasping his hands together, he took a deep breath and blurted out the speech he'd rehearsed more than a hundred times since Marie and Charles accepted his request to come visit.

"Mr. and Mrs. Jacobson—"

"Mom, Mimi, whichever you're comfortable with," Marie interrupted.

"Mom," Darren said and chuckled nervously.

"I love Kensi and I want to spend the rest of my life showing her. You have my word that I will honor and take care of her as long as there is breath in my body. So I came all the way here to ask if you would give me her hand in marriage."

Marie nodded enthusiastically as her eyebrows shot up. She was probably just as excited as Kensi should be, but Charles remained silent, watching Darren intently.

"Give me one reason why I should honor your request," Charles answered.

"Charles!" Marie exclaimed and slapped him on the shoulder, but he didn't budge and his eyes remained locked on Darren.

Darren was quiet for a moment, because he thought he'd explained that already. He loved Kensi and he wanted to be with her forever. Was that not enough?

"Other than the fact that I love her, I do believe that she is the answer to my prayers. Before meeting Kensi, I didn't think that I would ever love anyone this way again. I couldn't fathom getting married and sharing my life with anyone like this, but Kensi has come into my life to show me that love is possible when you're open. I believe that together, we can grow spiritually, mentally and emotionally. We complement each other. And I just don't want to go through life without her. Whatever life throws our way, we can make it through it as one. That is how much faith I have that God has brought us together." That was all Darren had to offer.

"You like to lay it on thick! Marie, don't be expecting nothing like that from me. He must read romance books or something . . . consider Kensi's yes, my yes," Charles confirmed with a handshake.

"Thank you, sir!"

Marie jumped up and threw her arms around Darren, nearly knocking the coffee mug out of Charles' hand. She kissed his cheek and exclaimed in her boisterous voice, "Welcome to the family!"

Darren's right ear rang from Marie's loud voice in his ear, but he ignored it. He was elated that he could finally ask Kensi to marry him. Waiting four more weeks to see Kensi was probably going to be one of the hardest things he had to do in a while. Who knew that pouring his all into working with the children in Pepperton would change his life in more ways than one? After Jessica died, he couldn't say that he fully trusted God's plans for his life, but seeing where His path had led him, Darren wholly embraced Jeremiah 29:11, *"For I know the plans I have for you," declares the Lord, "plans to prosper you and not to harm you, plans to give you hope and a future."* Though he'd had to endure some heartache, Darren was convinced that God's plans had proved to be far greater than anything he could have imagined.

Chapter 42

Darren scanned the baggage claim area for several minutes before locking eyes with the woman he'd been waiting to hold in his arms for the last several weeks. He advanced toward her as quickly as possible without running through the airport like a passenger who was about to miss a flight. In one full motion, he swooped her off her feet and held her securely in his arms for at least a minute before easing her feet back to the floor.

"I've been waiting on this moment since you dashed through the security gates in Pepperton. I've missed you," he professed, and without giving her a chance to respond, he placed his lips against hers. He pulled away when he felt a stray tear slide down her cheek, took one look at her and pulled her back into his arms again.

Kensi needed this, needed to be in Darren's arms, because there she found the comfort that she yearned for the last couple of weeks. Darren being there in that moment did more for her than he would ever know. Adam had been giving her the blues and making work very uncomfortable for her lately. He'd flip flop between payback and repentance, and it was driving her mad. He'd gone so far as to present her ideas as his own when it came to producing a digital newspaper. The worst part about it all was that she'd finally given in and talked to Samantha about it, and she did nothing. Kensi should have known that Samantha wouldn't do much, given their history. She clearly just wanted the job done, no matter who did it. As for Kensi, this set-up no longer worked. She was ready to turn in her resignation.

"What's wrong, Kens honey?" Darren asked. He grabbed his leather bag off the conveyor belt and they were on their way out of the airport. He held the bag in one hand and Kensi's hand in the other.

"We can talk about it later. I'm much better after seeing you. How was your flight?"

"Not bad. A little turbulence here and there but nothing too crazy. So, do we have an Uber, or will I have to endure more turbulence on the road to your place?"

"If you consider me your Uber, then yes. Didn't I get you to and fro in one piece last time? How quickly we forget!" Kensi reminded him teasingly, wagging her pointer finger in the air.

"I'll never forget praying for my life! You're worse than the taxi drivers, woman!"

"Well, you'll have to get used to it. It's either drive or get run over. Which do you prefer?"

"I guess I have no choice," Darren answered and tossed his bag into her trunk. He never failed to show his chivalrous side as he quickly reached past Kensi to get her door before making his way around to the passenger side.

"Help us, Father!"

"Really?" Kensi asked. Her mouth twisted into a scowl. "There are much worse drivers than me."

Darren's eyes widened as he slowly turned his attention to buckling his seatbelt and staring ahead.

"Tsk. Tsk. Little faith in my skills I see."

On the drive to Kensi's brownstone apartment, Darren said very little. He listened to Kensi vent about work happenings while he nodded and asked questions every now and again, but kept his eyes on the road.

"What's on the agenda for this evening?" Darren asked as he trailed behind her into her apartment.

"Another musical. Remember? We can get you checked into your hotel later."

"Yeah, I remember." For some reason Darren thought that would be tomorrow night, but was glad to know that they would have something to do besides spending time in her apartment. It also meant that he would be proposing one day earlier than he'd planned. Since she loved New York and the theater so much, he intended to propose at the box office.

They didn't have long to dress and make their way to see the Broadway show, *Shaken.* Kensi slipped into a little black dress that she'd purchased just for this event. The draped neckline and rouched side seam suited her perfectly. Darren's coordinated black single-breasted suit jacket and pants complimented her outfit effortlessly. His inside jacket pocket was perfect to conceal the small pearl-colored box.

They hailed a taxi to the theater district and walked a couple of blocks past the Winter Garden Theatre, Gershwin Theatre, and the August Wilson Theatre to the Broadway Theatre. Maybe it was because of the snow, but Darren didn't realize how much the entire area seemed so lively; it was intoxicating.

Kensi handed the passes to the attendant and they glided down the aisle until they arrived at the front row. Her stomach turned when she saw that Samantha and Adam would be occupying the seats next to theirs. She tried not to believe that Adam only chose to show up to spite her, because she wasn't one to believe in conspiracy theories. Him being there just didn't add up, but she refused to do the math that evening. She was there to enjoy the show with Darren.

Kensi politely spoke and introduced Darren to both Samantha and Adam and took special care to keep her attention directed toward Darren. Thankfully, Adam didn't go out of his way to get attention. He made a couple of comments about the show just loud enough for her to hear, but she chose not to comment.

Even if Darren had never encountered Adam previously, he would have noticed the tension between him and Kensi. Kensi had shared Adam's antics with him, so he was aware of the lack of professionalism around their office. He trusted Kensi to handle it, but would thoroughly enjoy a chance to check Adam once more. But just like Kensi, after speaking, he diverted his attention away from them. Tonight was all about him and Kensi.

The show opened with an original song written by Alicia Keys, one of Kensi's favorite artists. When the curtains opened, Darren didn't experience the goose bumps and tingling as he had when they saw *The Lion King* on Broadway, but it was impressive. The lights, costumes, music, dancing, singing, coupled with the story of a young amnesiac woman in search of finding her true self, made for a great show.

When the curtains closed and the crowd thinned out, Darren kneeled down on one knee and removed the pearl-colored box from his suit jacket.

"Kensi Marie Jacobson, you have been the best thing that has ever happened to me, an answered prayer. I want to spend the rest of my life getting to know you and growing old with you. With your parents' blessing, would you do me the honor of becoming Mrs. Darren Shaw?"

"Are you serious?"

"Indeed," he answered, popping open the box and showcasing the princess-cut diamond.

"Of course I will!"

Darren slipped the ring onto her ring finger, stood and pulled her into his arms. Those who stood around to watch the proposal and record it on their cell phones, cheered and congratulated the couple. Good thing she agreed, because his humiliation would have been plastered across social media in the next several seconds.

"I love you, Mr. Shaw!" Kensi murmured against his lips.

"I love you too, future Mrs. Shaw! Thank you for the best Valentine's Day gift this man could ask for."

"Just too bad you had to wait so long to get it."

"It was well worth the wait. You were worth the wait, Kensi. I love you so much and can't wait to spend the rest of my life showing you," Darren said before sealing their engagement with a kiss.

Chapter 43

Although Darren hated to leave Kensi behind, knowing that this would be the last time he'd have to make a trip to New York alone brought him an unspeakable amount of joy. And as much as Kensi loved New York, she began making arrangements the next morning to pack up and leave. The timing couldn't have been more perfect. Her lease was up at the end of next month, she was ready to leave her current position and Miss Sandra had all but offered her a job at *Pepperton Quad*.

She sauntered into the office on Monday morning and handed in her resignation to Samantha. She thanked her for the opportunities and agreed to finish any open assignments in Pepperton. Not once did Samantha try to talk her into staying, and that hurt a little, especially since she'd always told Kensi that she was her biggest cheerleader.

Kensi had grown to become sick of this place, and she had Adam and Samantha to thank for it. However, she thanked God for opening a door to get the experience she thought she always wanted. She had to admit that not getting the position at first dampened her faith, but actually taking the position reminded her more now than ever that God's will and timing is perfect.

It took her fifteen minutes to pack up her cubicle because she didn't bring many personal items into the office: a picture of her parents, a souvenir seashell from Mexico, and a couple of devotional books. She sifted through old files and tossed things to the trash that weren't relevant anymore.

"Are you sure you want to marry him?" Adam asked, his voice weak and wracked with emotion as he approached her cubicle from behind.

Kensi paused for a moment, but decided not to respond. Adam's myriad of emotions was not going to drive her crazy today. She wasn't even sure who the person was who was standing at her cubicle. He was certainly not the compassionate man she dated last year.

"I'm sorry about how I've been acting. Just think about all of this for a moment..." Kensi interrupted Adam. She didn't care to hear anything he had to say anymore.

"I love Darren—that's his name, by the way. And whatever this is you're doing, just please stop. Have a great life," Kensi responded. She lifted her box, maneuvered around him, leaving him standing at her cubicle, and walked to the elevator, praying that he didn't follow her. When she stepped on the elevator and turned around, she breathed a sigh of relief when she saw that the elevator bank was empty. Hopefully Adam would get some help so that he could have some peace, because she was at peace with her decisions.

∞

As pro New York as Kensi was, she never thought she'd be giving it up for love and a new life, but seeing the last piece of furniture on the moving van and turning in the keys to her brownstone apartment never felt so good. Her apartment in Pepperton was ready. All she needed to do was get there. She opted for a one-year lease while spending the next year wedding planning.

This time last year, she was beginning to think that she couldn't have both the career and love she desired, but now she had everything she'd ever wanted. It just didn't come in the package she was looking for or when she thought it would.

After changing planes in Houston and riding the cropduster into Pepperton, she had to laugh at her circumstance. Arriving into Pepperton the first time, she thought it was the end of her life, but it was the start of a new chapter.

"Welcome Home My Love!" Tears of joy streamed down her face seeing the sign that Darren stood in the middle of baggage claim holding.

"Okay, who helped you with this sign?" Kensi greeted after pulling out of Darren's embrace.

"All that matters is that it's true," he answered and tossed the sign to the floor, pulled her into his arms and properly welcomed her in a way that no sign ever could.

Thank you

Thank you for your support! I hope you enjoyed Kensi's story, please let me know what you think! E-mail me, post a review to Amazon and/or Goodreads, or give me a shout-out on social media! If you haven't read any of the Love, Lies & Consequences series, I encourage you to purchase your copies and enjoy! Until next time!

About the author

In addition to reading and writing, Natasha enjoys reading, cooking, couponing, and spending her time with her husband and children. She has won the Readers' Choice award for her books, *The Life Your Spirit Craves*, *Love, Lies & Consequences, and The Life Your Spirit Craves for Mommies*.

Natasha believes that we were all created for purpose and inspires women to pursue their God-given purpose through her books and the How Long Are You Going to Wait Conference. Sign up for her monthly newsletter at www.natashafrazier.com for encouraging devotionals, current events and new releases.

Connect with Natasha:

Instagram @author_natashafrazier

Facebook @craves.2012

Twitter @author_natashaf

e-mail: Natasha@natashafrazier.com